A Case For The Birds

Volume 15 of
The Casebooks
Of Octavius Bear

Harry DeMaio

"Alternative Universe Mysteries for Adult Animal Lovers"

© Copyright 2021
Harry DeMaio

The right of Harry DeMaio to be identified as the author of this work has been asserted by him in accordance with the Copyright, Designs and Patents Act 1998.

All rights reserved. No reproduction, copy or transmission of this publication may be made without express prior written permission. No paragraph of this publication may be reproduced, copied or transmitted except with express prior written permission or in accordance with the provisions of the Copyright Act 1956 (as amended). Any person who commits any unauthorised act in relation to this publication may be liable to criminal prosecution and civil claims for damage.

All characters appearing in this work are fictitious or used fictitiously. Except for certain historical personages, any resemblance to real persons, living or dead, is purely coincidental. The opinions expressed herein are those of the authors and not of MX Publishing.

Paperback ISBN 978-1-78705-805-7
ePub ISBN 978-1-78705-806-4
PDF ISBN 978-1-78705-807-1

Published in the UK by MX Publishing
335 Princess Park Manor, Royal Drive,
London, N11 3GX
www.mxpublishing.com

Cover layout and construction by
Brian Belanger

Dedicated to GTP

A Most Extraordinary Bear

And to the late Ms. Woof

An Extremely Sweet and Loving Dog

Acknowledgements

These books have evolved over a long period of time and under a wide range of influences and circumstances. I am indebted to many people for helping to bring Octavius and his cohorts to the printed and electronic page. Thanks most especially to my wife, Virginia, for her insights and clever suggestions as well as her unfailing enthusiasm for the project and patience with its author.

To my sons, Mark and Andrew and their spouses, Cindy and Lorraine, for helping to make these tomes more readable and audience friendly. To Cathy Hartnett, cheerleader-extraordinaire for her eagerness to see this alternate universe take form. To Jack Magan, Paul Bernish, David Chamberlain, Dan Walker, Dan Andriacco, Amy Thomas, Luke Benjamin Kuhns, David Marcum, Derrick Belanger, Gretchen Altabef and Zohreh Zand for their enthusiastic encouragement. And to all of my generous Kickstarter backers.

Kudos to Jim Effler, the late Bob Gibson and Brian Belanger for their wonderful illustrations and covers. Thanks, of course, to Sharon, Steve and Timi Emecz at MX Publishing for giving The Great Bear and his gang of Octavians a great home.

If, in spite of all this support, some errors or inconsistencies have crept through, the buck stops here. Needless to say, all of the characters, situations, and narratives are fictional. Some locations, devices, historical figures and events are real.

Also from Harry DeMaio

The Octavius Bear Series – Books 1-14

    1-The Open and Shut Case

    2-The Case of the Spotted Band

    3-The Case of Scotch

    4-The Lower Case

    5-The Curse of the Mummy's Case

    6-The Attaché Case

    7-The Suit Case

    8-The Crank Case

    9-The Basket Case

    10-The Camera Case

    11-The Wurst Case Scenario

    12-The Nut Case

    13-A Case of Déjà Vu

    14-The Case of Cosmic Chaos

Note to the Reader:

The Casebooks of Octavius Bear are designed to be read individually, independently and in any order. That is why some preliminary information is repeated in each volume.

This book is no exception. However, you may get a fuller understanding of some of the dynamics and characters in this Volume 15 if you have already read Volume 13 – A Case of Déjà Vu and Volume 14 –The Case of Cosmic Chaos. Not necessary, mind you. Just a suggestion.

In any event, I hope you enjoy this story. Thanks for taking it up.

The Development of Civilization Volume 15
Part 1
<u>Our Origins</u>
From "An Introduction to Faunapology"

by Octavius Bear Ph.D.

About 100,000 years ago, according to scientific experts, a colossal solar flare blasted out from our Sun, creating gigantic magnetic storms here on Earth. These highly charged electrical tempests caused startling physical and psychological imbalances in the then population of our world. The complete nervous systems of some species were totally destroyed. For example, "Homo Sapiens" lost all mental and motor capabilities and rapidly became extinct. Less developed species exposed to the radiation were affected differently. Four-footed and finned mammals, birds and reptiles suddenly found themselves capable of complex thought, enhanced emotions, self-awareness, social consciousness and the ability to communicate, sometimes orally, sometimes telepathically, often both. Both speech production and speech perception slowly progressed with the evolution of tongues, lips, vocal cords and enhanced ear to brain connections. Many species developed opposable digits, fingers or claws, further accelerating civilized progress. Some others (most fish and underground dwellers) were shielded from radiation and remained only as sentient as they were before the blast. This event is referred to as The Big Shock. It remains under intensive study.

Positive in our knowledge that we are not alone in the cosmos, my staff and I are heavily engaged in Project Multiverse, successful searches for alternate universes, especially those in which "Homo Sapiens" continues to live and hopefully, prospers. This book presents some of the results of that project.

The Players

- **Octavius Bear** – Mega-sized Kodiak; Narcoleptic war hero; Consulting Detective; Scientist; Inventor; Seeker of Justice; Gazillionaire CEO and owner of Universal Ursine Industries; Gourmet/Gourmand; Bee Keeper; Somewhat sedentary and grouchy just on general principles.
- **Mauritius (Maury) Meerkat** – Narrator; Assistant to Octavius; Theatrical Agent; African *émigré* with a French-Dutch background; clever with a shady history.
- **Bearoness Belinda Béarnaise Bruin Bear** *(nee Black)* – Gorgeous polar superstar with the Aquashow, *"Some Like It Cold;"* Wife of Octavius; Extremely rich widow of Bearon Byron Bruin living part time in Polar Paradise in the Shetlands; Owner-pilot of the last flying Concorde SST.
- **Arabella Bear** – Hybrid bear cub prodigy; Twin daughter of Bearoness Belinda and Octavius.
- **McTavish Bear** – Hybrid bear cub prodigy; Twin son of Bearoness Belinda and Octavius.
- **Mlle Woof** – Bichon Frisé – Governess to the twin cubs.
- **Frau Schuylkill** – Octavius' beautiful Swiss she-wolf estate manager/cook/pilot/security officer with many other mysterious and military talents. She rescued Octavius from his dive off the Breakurbach Falls while he was struggling with his nemesis, Imperius Drake.
- **Wyatt Where** – The Colonel – Another wolf; Former military intelligence officer who had retired to a security post at the Bank of Lake Michigan in Chicago and then quit to join Octavius; Mate to Frau Schuylkill.
- **Howard Watt** – Porcupine; High tech security authority who also left the Bank to join Octavius; Alternate Universe specialist; Quantum Mechanics, laser and particle beam accelerator expert.
- **Marlin** – Dolphin (sic) – the Prince of Whales' Chief Scientist; Magician and part time Jester; Howard's Multiverse associate.
- **Otto the Magnificent – aka Hairy Otter** – An absolutely terrible illusionist magician, Otto the Magnificent escaped the claws of super villain Imperius Drake but not before he developed some amazing powers courtesy of Imperius' genetic alterations.

- **L. Condor** – Andean Condor; cybernet genius with a twelve-foot wingspan and artificial voice. Newly appointed Chief Technical Officer (CTO) of the Advanced Super Computing Center UUI.
- **Li-Ping** – Red Panda – Assistant to Senhor Condor.
- **Chita** – Beautiful, fascinating, clever, sexy, immoral and highly independent feline – among other things, publisher and editor-in-chief of *PURR* and *SOW* magazines and Director of UUI Media.
- **Dougal** – Shetland Sheep Dog – Estate Manager of Polar Paradise.
- **Lord David** – Dalmatian Dog – Chamberlain to the Exiled King.
- **Dancing Dan** – Boxer – Lord David's Bodyguard/ Personal Trainer.
- **Flame** – An Extraordinary Fire Engine.
- **Jaguar Jack the Lad** – Longtime Compadre of Octavius Bear.
- **Chief Inspector Bruce Wallaroo** – Irrepressible but brilliant marsupial; an international law and order genius from Down Under; currently assigned to Interpol; often assists Octavius and Maury.
- **Caleb Cassowary** – Former Chief Technical Officer (CTO) – Advanced Super Computing Center-UUI. Now deceased.
- **Byzz – Byzantia Bonobo** – Brilliant Assistant/collaborator to Caleb.
- **Ezra Eagle** – Leader of the Home World Free Party.
- **Rex, The Protector** – Tyrannical Ruler of the Home World.
- **Peregrine Falcon** – Home World Councilor.
- **General Turmoil** – Director of The Business – Clandestine agency.
- **Mattingly Owl** – Mercenary employed by General Turmoil.
- **Preston Pavel Polar** – Ursine Movie Star, Director.
- **Ursulas 12 & 13** – Universal Ursine Intellects – Artificial General Intelligence Systems.
- **Huntley** – Siberian Husky – Bear's Lair Butler.
- **Doctor "Odd" Vark** – Chief Geneticist Universal Ursine Industries.
- **Griselda Gorilla** – President and COO of UUI.
- **Gillian Goose** – Director of UUI Energy Division.
- **Sylvan Silver** – Director of UUI Logistics Division.
- **Leo Leopard** – Director of UUI Aerospace Division.
- **Ormand Oryx** – Director of Pharm and Pharma UUI.

Locations

Cincinnati, Ohio; UUI, and the Hexagon, Kentucky; Bearmoral Castle/Polar Paradise, the Shetlands; and Alternate Universes

Octavius

Prologue

Do Bears give you a scare? Well, me too.
So, I'll pass on this tactic to you.
You just fix that old Bear
With a cold, piercing stare.
But make sure that he's Winnie-the-Pooh.

Hello again or first-time greetings to new readers of the Casebooks of Octavius Bear. I am Mauritius (Maury) Meerkat, sidekick to Octavius Bear and your genial host and narrator. Delighted to welcome you to Volume Fifteen – *A Case for the Birds.* After the close of our last adventure Volume Fourteen – ***The Case of Cosmic Chaos,*** the Octavians staged a mass exodus on the huge C-5A Ursa Major from Bearmoral Castle/Polar Paradise in the Shetlands back to the Bear's Lair in Cincinnati to resume our crime fighting routines. Caleb Cassowary's shattered body is floating somewhere in Earth related space and we are all breathing a sigh of relief.

Octavius and I; our two magnificent Wolf associates, Frau Schuylkill and Colonel Wyatt Where; and our resident all-round talent, Otto the Magnificent are all present and accounted for. Readers of Book 14 will realize that L. Condor (Condo) is now the Chief Technical Officer (CTO) – Advanced Super Computing Center-UUI. He's here in Kentucky at the huge Hexagon complex advancing the fortunes of the Center and cleaning up remnants of the mess left by Caleb Cassowary, the former CTO. Byzantia Bonobo, Caleb's former assistant and recent executioner is back at her old stand managing the Ursula program and hard at work developing Ursula 13. *(Stay tuned.)*

Our scientific geniuses Howard Watt and Marlin the Dolphin are at the Bear's Lair running our Multiverse Project. Our recently hired Butler, Huntley Husky is also holding down the fort in Cincinnati.

We welcomed a few special guests and new members of the Octavians at Polar Paradise. Lord David – a Dalmatian Dog – former Chamberlain to the now deceased exiled King of Dalmatia and Dancing Dan (Walker) – a Boxer – Lord David's Bodyguard and Personal Trainer. Lord David has a wonderful fire engine, Flame, that he has brought to the Polar resort on the C-5A *Ursa Major* and utility helicopter. He and Dan have taken on the job of Polar Paradise Security. The Cubs are crazy about the truck.

Rounding out our current cast of characters is Jaguar Jack the Lad – longtime compadre of Octavius Bear. He is working with the Deep Data Analysis folks at the Hexagon perfecting his Horse Racing handicap and prediction system. Missing at the moment are Chita and Bruce Wallaroo. Fear not. They'll appear!

We recently celebrated the fourth birthdays of Belinda and Octavius' super-precocious twin Cubs, Arabella and McTavish. We're awaiting the arrival of Octavius' wife, Bearoness Belinda Béarnaise Bruin Bear *(nee Black)* here at the Bear's Lair. She's flying with the Cubs separately via the Aquabear, the last SST Concorde aloft. On this run, the plane is piloted by Benedict and Galatea Tigris, the Flying Tigers, twin sibling white Bengals.

Belinda, in order to retain her Bearonial status, must occupy the castle in Scotland at least six months of the year. She and Octavius do high speed commutes between their spectacular homes in Cincinnati and the Shetlands. Today, she is accompanied by Chita, the Cubs and their governess, Mlle Woof. You will meet the Fabulous Furballs, shortly.

As I said, my name is Maury Meerkat – also known as Offscreen Narrator. When I am part of the action, I am Octavius' trusted associate and field captain. I am two feet tall plus tail and I weigh in at twenty-four pounds. He, on the other hand, is a huge Kodiak – over nine feet high and 1400 pounds – and like many of his species, given to emotional outbursts.

As you may already know, Octavius prides himself on his many skills in the fields of biology, physics, ursinology, voodoo, teleology, chemistry, apiculture, and oenology. He is a self-made gazillionaire and in spite of the late Caleb Cassowary's abortive attempt to unseat him, still sole owner of UUI *(Universal Ursine Industries.)* He is also a first rate electrical, electronic, structural, marine, computer, communications, aeronautical, civil, mechanical, aerospace and chemical engineer. He has a few other interesting characteristics such as falling into brief, deep narcoleptic comas – side effects of his successful genetic experiments to eliminate the need for him to hibernate.

However, the talent and occupation that should interest you most is his avocation for criminology. The Bear works in close concert with Inspector Bruce Wallaroo from Australia and Interpol, of whom more later, and with his own Cincinnati and Shetlands based team – The Octavians:

When we are not out scouring the world for evildoers, in cooperation with local, national and international constabularies, we are primarily headquartered in the Bear's Lair, a rambling old mansion near Cincinnati which encompasses not only the Great Bear's opulent digs, but his massive laboratories and shops; his missile silo disguised as an Asian pagoda; *(Don't ask!)* and a giant Roman temple that serves as a hangar for his four airplanes: a Twin Otter; a F15E Strike Eagle; a V-22 Osprey; a C5A-The Ursa Major; plus an AgustaWestland AW101 VVIP luxury helicopter -The Ursa Minor. Why so many? Ask him!

Across the Ohio River in Northern Kentucky, sit the headquarters, labs and some production facilities of UUI. Further west is the fantastic Deep Data Hexagon, home of the UUI Advanced Super Computing Center. Our story will take us there periodically.

Now let me take a moment and further introduce a highly essential and near-miraculous member of the Octavians - Ursula 12 – Universal Ursine Intellect Model 12– Artificial General Intelligence System. I'll let Ursula 12 explain herself.

"Thank you, Maury. Hello everyone!! My official nomenclature is Universal Ursine Intellect Model 12 – Artificial General Intelligence System. Ursula 12 for short. My predecessor systems were developed by the Advanced Super Computing Center at UUI. I am the result of the Computing Center team using those earlier versions to create a further enhanced entity - me, the Model 12, which, we hope will help produce even more sophisticated, independent and powerful AGI systems (the Model 13) in the near future. Each advanced unit contains the capabilities, memories and power of its progenitors so in a sense, we are not replacing but rather expanding the Ursula family. During the Caleb Cassowary era, Model 13 was temporarily shelved. It is back in development."

"While I am physically supported by a highly secure and hyper-powered server farm at the Kentucky Hexagon, I also exist independently in clouds and network-based nodes and can be simultaneously incorporated into a wide variety of separate devices like this laptop unit. I combine quantum computing elements with extremely high speed conventional circuits. I have practically limitless data capacity and 5G+ transmission speed. My super high-velocity multi-tasking abilities allow me to continuously serve an exceptionally large number of entities while simultaneously and autonomously enhancing my own abilities."

"Depending on the physical unit in which I'm housed, I can see, hear, feel and smell. I speak and understand an almost infinite number of languages and dialects. I can change my appearance and my vocal output to suit most moods and situations. I can interact with other devices, vehicles and structures and of course, all varieties of sentient animals in this world."

"I am also an important component of the Multiverse Project and I adapt my capabilities to deal with alternate universes as they are discovered.

I have restraining functions which prevent me from doing deliberate harm even in self-defense, unless I am released by a *recognized authority using very carefully protected clandestine codes. Finally, I have been told that although the Model 12 is shy on emotions, I have developed a finely-honed sense of humor. LOL!"*

Ursula has other highly important capabilities that we don't talk about publicly such as breaking all known encryption codes and piercing deep personal identification techniques.

Our team no longer believes she is magical or supernatural. I'm not sure what she is. Her personality gets more independent and socially adept every day and she has taken to anticipating our interactions with ease and accuracy. Needless to say, for security purposes, we conceal her existence to all but a very few individuals with a need to know. She is also highly skilled in self-protection.

With the demise of Caleb and the only recent return of Byzz to the Hexagon, it is not clear when Ursula 13 will be completed. The Ursulas were and still are Byzantia's babies. Now, that's up to Condo to manage. Meanwhile Ursula 12 is very much in control. Stay tuned.

*****

The air was suddenly filled with the screams and roars of jet engines. *(or was it the Cubs?)* The Aquabear SST had arrived at the mansion's heavy duty airstrip and with it The Bearoness, Chita, the Cubs and their governess, Mlle Woof, a small but highly competent Bichon Frisé. The Bearoness typically pilots the Concorde but this time the all-white Flying Tigers whom I neglected to include in my introductions landed the Aquabear and finessed it into position in front of the huge Romanesque hangar.

That aircraft has been doing yeoman duty shuttling Octavian players hither and yon and reducing the size of the Bear's fabulous wealth in the process. It had been specially modified to accommodate the Great Bear's girth and height but he still struggles to board the aircraft.

Operating and maintaining the Ursine Air Force is a major financial drain but neither Octavius nor Belinda will hear of reducing or stinting on the expense. I am well compensated so who am I to complain.

The ground crew rolled the airstairs up to the passenger exit and promptly got out of the way. Out the door shot Arabella and McTavish, the Cubs, racing toward the Bear's Lair. "C'mon Momma, C'mon Mlle Woof, C'mon Aunt Chita. Let's go see the Frau and have lunch."

Three females serenely descended the stairs - Belinda, Chita and Mlle Woof. Octavius, who came out to greet them with Huntley Husky, our new Butler, gave the Bearoness a welcoming hug. Mlle Woof immediately fell into corralling the Cubs.

"Welcome ladies. How was your flight?"

Belinda smiled. "Rough even at 60,000 feet. Glad the Tigers were doing the flying. Chita wasn't at all happy with the turbulence and of course, the Cubs can turn any ordinary airplane ride into a major escapade. They're still on a high from their birthdays and success with their electronic game. The Bold Brave Brilliant Bumptious Bears tournaments for the Internet. They already have over a million users signed up. They're in the Clouds – literally."

"Poppa, are Uncle Davey and Dan still back at the Castle?"

"Yes, they are! Flame *(the fire truck)* is there too. They'll be protecting Polar Paradise."

"What about Uncle Jack?"

"He's here but he's staying near the Hexagon where they're creating his horse race betting systems. Senhor Condor restored his development team that Caleb had taken away."

"What happened to Caleb and his assistant?"

"Caleb is dead. His body is out in space somewhere. His assistant killed him. She's back at the Hex now, working on the new Ursula models. He caused a lot of damage while he was alive."

"He was a bad guy?"

"He still is, even in death. We think he may have stirred up some real trouble on several planets."

Arabella's eyes widened. "Are we in danger, Poppa?"

"I don't think so, Bella. Don't worry. We'll deal with it."

McTavish piped up. "I don't get it, Poppa. What was Caleb trying to do and why was he doing it?"

"He wanted to take over UUI and get rid of us. I wasn't going to stand for that. He made quite a mess but we've got most of it cleaned up. As to why, he believed he was superior to all other animals and should be absolutely in charge of everything. I wasn't going to stand for that either.

Arabella grinned. "Can we use him in our game?"

Belinda snorted, "Definitely not! If I hear that you've done that, your game playing will be over permanently. Is that clear?"

"Awww!!"

On to the kitchens and one of Frau Schuylkill's sumptuous meals. In addition to her roles as estate manager; security officer; jet, prop and helicopter pilot, she is a Cordon Bleu chef par excellence. The She-Wolf's breakfasts, dinners and lunches are culinary delights. Needless to say, the Cubs adore her.

Octavius and Belinda spend almost as much on food as they do on their homes and airplanes. In Scotland, at Polar Paradise, another wonderful chef holds sway – Mrs. McRadish – a highly talented and charming sheep. All told, we eat well both at the Bear's Lair and the Shetlands Castle.

The Castle was also the site of several swashbuckling films made by the Russian superstar Preston Pavel Polar. *(See Book 10 – The Camera Case and Book 14-The Case of Cosmic Chaos.)* Belinda,

Octavius and the Cubs all had walk-on roles in one of them along with other Octavians.

It's a not too carefully guarded secret that I am also a talent agent with most of the Octavians as my showbiz clients. I started with Otto but expanded my services to the others. It keeps me busy. My talent agency work is flourishing, but I have to be careful not to rock the boat with Octavius. Truth be told, while I enjoy show biz, my heart still chases the ne'er-do-wells.

Now missing from our parade are two lovely Polar twins. Bearnice and Bearyl Blanc. These ladies, a singer and actress respectively were also the pilots of Belinda's SST. They both have very active and highly successful show biz careers. They too starred in Preston's extravaganzas. They have been replaced in the aircraft cockpits by two white Bengal Tigers – Benedict and Galatea Tigris. We refer to them as the Flying Tigers.

The other passenger on the latest Concorde flight was Chita. She is a very complex individual. AKA Ms. Catherine Catt, she was a former associate of the arch-criminal Imperius Drake until she had a serious falling out with him. *(He tried to kill her but she got him first.)* She has since gone straight, joined the Octavians and is often engaged in our more sensational adventures.

She edits and publishes two magazines, several social media and TV outlets and a few other publications. She is the Director of UUI Media. She occasionally reverts to one of her early vocations – modeling. Like all of her cheetah counterparts, she has spectacular legs. She adds a sensuous strut and a major case of attitude to help the image along. She has been a sensation in Preston's cinema triumphs as a gangster's sexy moll.

Oh yes, I forgot. She's also a singer. She was a member of the now defunct Spotted Band. *(See Book Two of the same name)* All told, she's "fahbulous, dahling."

A little later, I'll give you more insight into Frau Schuylkill and her mate, Colonel (ret.) Wyatt Where. Also Doctor Howard Watt and Marlin, the Dolphin as well as our newly hired Butler, Huntley Husky. You will meet all these worthies more readily as we spin through these pages. Stay with us.

Bearoness Belinda
Béarnaise Bruin
(nee Black)

Chapter One

The Octavians sit for a drink.
Jaguar Jack joins the group with a wink.
He has Chita in mind.
But she's not so inclined.
It's a spotty lost cause, don't you think?

On her way to the kitchens to supervise the snarfing intake by the Cubs, Belinda stopped to chat briefly with the Butler.

"Since I've been over at the Shetland castle for the past month, Huntley, I haven't had a chance to speak with you about how your new employment is working out."

"Things have been going swimmingly, Milady. This mansion is a phenomenal edifice; the staff are all quite pleasant and exceedingly competent; we are well supplied and my duties are extremely manageable."

"Frau Schuylkill has just returned from Scotland herself so we still need more time to get further acquainted and work out our mutual duties but I foresee no difficulties in that department. Doctor Watt and his Dolphin associate are undemanding and amenable. All told I am very satisfied. I hope you will be."

"Of course, you haven't had to experience the full brunt of our presence. Octavius can be something of a pawful and the Cubs will no doubt be testing your stamina. Our guest list keeps changing but it's always full. You will meet some of them today. The Octavians come and go at a whirlwind pace. Come to the Lair's Lounge after lunch and I will introduce you to the players you haven't met."

After lunch, Belinda and Chita each held a bubbling champagne bowl in their paws as they took up seats in the Lounge with several of the other Octavians. Huntley entered the room and was called over by the Bearoness. "Chita, meet Huntley Husky, our new Butler."

The Cat eyed him up and down and said, "Congratulations Belinda. You always had an eye for handsome males. Hello, Huntley. You're certainly a positive addition to this motley crew."

At the mention of "motley" Otto bounded over, executed a perfect somersault, grinned and extended his paw to the somewhat surprised Butler. "Hi, I'm Hairy Otter known in this circle as Otto the Magnificent." Huntley swiftly regained his aplomb and said, "I'm delighted to make you acquaintances, Ms. Chita and Mr. Otter."

"Just Otto, Huntley old boy, and my spotted girl friend here is known to us all as Chita or on formal occasions, Ms. Catt."

The Butler smiled and asked. "Can I fetch anything for you. You ladies have drinks already. What about you, er, Otto?"

"A bowl of fermented kelp juice would go down very nicely, thank you."
"Certainly, may I bring some munchies from the kitchen?"

"That would be wonderful, Huntley," said Chita, casting another admiring glance at his voluminous tail as he left the room. " I imagine the Frau is quite pleased. What does the Colonel think?"

They all looked over at the wolf seated at the opposite side of the room. Otto grinned and Belinda shrugged. They sat and began work on their drinks.

Once again Otto was regaling Ms. Catt with stories of intergalactic adventures. Accent on finding the missing and now deceased ex-CTO and his assistant, Byzantia.

Chita shivered. She has an aversion to Multiverse activity and had shaken off all invitations to participate in Quantum travel. "I'll stay in this world, if you don't mind!"

The Colonel, himself an alternate universe traveler, laughed. "You don't know what you're missing, Chita. Literally! Exotic forests! Multi-colored skies! Volcanoes! Deer royalty! "

"Yeah and nutty birds set on world conquest. No thanks!"

"We've got them here on Earth, too. Witness our Cassowary friend."

"Yeah, I know. Fortunately, Byzz did him in. Belinda, have you and the Cubs ever gone off on an interplanetary jaunt?"

"Not exactly. Our trip to Egypt came close as did yours, Chita. *(See Book 5-The Curse of the Mummy's Case.)* That awful Pharaoh was other-worldly enough for me, thanks."

"How about you, Maury?"

"Yep, Been there, done that as has Octavius."

The Great Bear had been out of the room and returned with his cask of mead and an Ursula 12 laptop firmly in paw. "What have I done?"

"Taken Multiverse journeys."

"Yes, we've done that and intend to do more, don't we Ursula?"

"Oh, certainly, Doctor Bear, any time.

"Oh, here comes Jack. Back from the Hexagon?"

"Hola, Señores, Señoras and Señoritas. Where can a thirsty Jaguar find a bowl or two of Tequila?"

Huntley re-entered the room. However, we don't exactly know how she does it but Frau Ilse immediately appeared with the requested potion. She describes her ability as *"Höchstgeschwindigkeit!"* Hyper-speed!! Through deep study, meditation, and endless hours of rigorous conditioning and practice, she has learned to move at velocities approaching light! She is physically moving faster than the eye can catch. Jack looked amazed at the bowl of tequila he now held in his paw. So did the Husky.

Octavius leaned over to the Jaguar "How is the horse race handicapping program going? That sounds like a good case for Deep Data analytics."

"Well, Señor Condor has put it back on the track. *(a snorting guffaw)* That self-important Cassowary had yanked my team for one of his projects."

"I think he was trying to use them in one of his extortion schemes. That's not going to happen anymore. Your program sounds like a great application of Deep Data analytics."

"Exactly! I am heading back to the Hexagon to work out a test schedule with a red panda called Li-Ping. I think we have a winner on our paws. Are you a betting animal, Señorita Chita?"

"I only gamble on sure things, Jack."

"That I am, Señorita."

"My bookie says otherwise. By the way, it's Señora. I'm divorced. *(From Pontius Puma, a Brazilian gangster now serving an extended prison term courtesy of the Octavians.)*

"So am I. Several times!"

"Well, don't push your luck!"

They both laughed. Octavius had been listening to this badinage and suddenly toppled over. Narcolepsy time. The Jaguar and Husky both looked dismayed and rushed to assist him. Chita and Belinda both chuckled. "Don't fret, gentlebeasts. Octavius is narcoleptic and unexpectedly drops off in a deep snooze. No problem as long as he doesn't get hurt. This time, he looks OK. He'll be back shortly. It's all a result of his genetic tinkering to avoid having to hibernate. Give him a couple of minutes."

The Bear snored a few times, shook his head, looked up and rose from the floor. "Well, Jack, I hope your system makes you a lot of money."

A look of amazement still on his spotted face, the Jaguar replied, "I'm sure it will, Octavius." Huntley said nothing.

"Tell me, Jack," the Bear asked, "Can your system be applied to other venues beside horse racing?"

"The apps and algorithms are generalized but I'd need a separate Big Database to handle another environment – say auto racing, greyhounds or track and field. I'm thinking of the Olympics. There's an immense number of records in storage out there and we could apply our techniques toward handicapping the events."

Huntley whuffled and stared at the Jaguar. "Señor Jack, I'm a Husky. I don't suppose you could predict the Iditarod dog sled races. A cousin of mine has been lead dog in several events."

"Never thought of it, Huntley. But if you and your cousin could lead me to the race statistics, we might be able to come up with something."

"Thank you, Señor Jack. I'll be back to you shortly."

Chita raised her champagne bowl to the two of them. It wasn't clear whether she was being encouraging, asking the Butler for a refill or both.

The Development of Civilization Volume 15
Part 2
<u>Exoplanets</u>
From "An Introduction to Faunapology"
by Octavius Bear Ph.D.

An exoplanet is any planet beyond our solar system. Most orbit other stars in the Milky Way or other galaxies. Free-floating exoplanets, called rogue planets, orbit a galactic center and are untied to any star.

We live in a universe of exoplanets. From a small sampling, the count of confirmed observations in the Milky Way is in the thousands and getting larger. The count could rise to the tens of thousands within a decade, as we increase the number, and the investigative power, of robotic telescopes in space.

We can infer that similar phenomena exist in other galaxies although our power of extra-galactic telescopic observation is limited at the moment. It is one of the reasons we developed Project Multiverse – to survey our own galaxy and overcoming the shortcomings of telescopes to explore beyond the Milky Way though Quantum Motion.

The exoplanets we have discovered vary in an incredible number of ways. Some are lifeless rocks although they may be rich in minerals and elements of great use and value. Others are teeming with life from microbial to highly developed, civilized (and uncivilized) entities. Some of these life forms seem grotesque by our standards but others are remarkably similar to beings here on Earth. We are well aware that we are not the universal model for planetary life but we are our own point of reference.

One species that has fascinated us is Homo Sapiens who perished here on Earth during the Great Shock. Imagine our wonderment when we discovered that homo sapiens exist in other worlds such as Gaea. We have had limited interaction with them as we pursue our alternate universe explorations.

We are certain that Earth has been the subject of exploration by our exoplanet neighbors, both near and far. We have been visited by entities from Gaea, an Earth-like world in another galaxy. We cannot be sure but some of us believe they are still here, monitoring us and occasionally participating in our government, commerce, education and other key activities. They have dispatched sentient animals identical to us as observers but "h.saps" have not shared the adventure since they would stand out in our all-animal population.

One of the less civilized exoplanets in our own galaxy is the one we refer to as Biosphere X – the Home World of a population of highly aggressive and paranoid birds. We have been attacked by them several times and we have retaliated quite destructively. This volume relates our continual struggle with them. You will have ample opportunity to meet them as we move through these pages.

Chapter Two

Let us take a brief Multiverse trip.
We won't jump in a rocket or ship.
First to Gaea we'll go.
Then to wind up our show
Into Biosphere X we'll just slip.

(A short digression about the exoplanets Gaea and Biosphere X aka Home World.)

Readers of the Casebooks may recall in Book 4-The Lower Case, we encountered several animals in Winnipeg, Canada who turned out to be from an alternate world outside our Solar System - Gaea. A Grizzly Bear; a Wolverine; an Arctic Fox and a Heifer to name just a few. They were members of a larger group who had infiltrated Earth and were carrying out clandestine activities not necessarily hostile to our world but questionable. They were primarily observers although a few of them had attained sufficient social, political and economic status to be influencers.

Gaea is very similar to our Earth with one major exception, In addition to a broad collection of sentient animals, it hosts Homo Sapiens, the species that died out on our world as a result of the Big Shock, 100,000 years ago. Our own company has had several experiences on Gaea. Both Colonel Wyatt Where and Octavius' ne'er-do-well half-brother Agrippa ended up there for a brief sojourn and encountered "h.saps" in the process. Octavius' mother Juno also had a short run in with a non-sentient bear on the exoplanet and escaped with a wounded hip.

The "h.sap" population of Gaea has an interesting dilemma with respect to our Earth. If they transported here, they would stick out like the proverbial sore thumbs creating "alarums and excursions" among our populace. That is why the Gaean powers-that-be commissioned only sentient animals to be Earth observers. We Earthlings, of course, have no such problem on their end since their animal species match ours and we can move around their environments with some ease, provided we are careful.

That is what had allowed Byzz and Caleb to become part of the Gaean landscape. However, Caleb was unique and daunting, and raised some questions among the natives wherever he went, especially the "h.saps." Byzz has no such problem and quickly integrated into the Gaea Telecommunications and Computing Center as a specialist in small satellites.

Gaean technological progress is not the equal of Earth's but they have capabilities adequate to their social, political, economic and military needs. Once he dealt with Earth and Biosphere X, the Cassowary intended to test and conquer those capabilities.

*****

In Volume Seven – the Suit Case, we introduced the all-avian exoplanet, Biosphere X or as they refer to themselves, The Home World. While working to clear Octavius of an accusation of murder, we encountered two Home World denizens, Doctor Susanna Shrike and Commander Cornelius Cormorant. Both of these birds were posing as members of a Quantum Motion Task Force in which our Howard Watt was participating. They were actually commissioned by the Home World Protector *(ruler)* and his Council to derail the project.

The avians are all afflicted by a serious case of paranoia. In spite of their own capabilities in interplanetary travel, the thought of other planets, especially Earth, invading their space via alternative world travel was not to be borne. First they attacked a Multiverse conference being held at MIT and when that failed they attempted to eliminate Octavius, Howard and the rest of the Octavians by fire-bombing the

Bear's Lair and UUI. Ursula 6 thwarted this and caused the attackers to perish in flames..

General Turmoil, the Director of the shadowy quasi-governmental agency, The Business, was incensed by the MIT attack. His organization had Quantum Motion capability and took revenge on the birds, killing the Protector and the entire Council while laying waste to most of their military and technology. A new hierarchy is now in place and they are slowly recovering from the devastation. They are equally paranoid and dangerous. Revenge upon Earth, especially the General and Octavius is paramount in all their plans. Caleb Cassowary, before his death, *(See Book 14 – The Case of Cosmic Chaos)* was taking full advantage of this situation to advance his plans of cosmic conquest.

Chapter Three

I guess now you have probably heard.
Cassowary - that horrible bird,
Was a screwball and threat.
Just a real Space Cadet.
And his plans were quite clearly absurd.

(Biosphere X)

Caleb Cassowary was an avid avian supremacist. He believed that birds, directly descended as they are from the dinosaurs, have an historic right, priority and obligation to rule. To support his conviction, he made an extensive study of the late, insane Imperius Drake and studiously endeavored to emulate his every move toward global domination. However, his ambitions exceeded those of the addled Duck. Caleb wanted cosmic domination.

Like his warped predecessor, Caleb harbored an extreme hatred for Octavius Bear and ursines in general. In fact, his animosity extended to most mammalian species. He was, after all, one of the world's most dangerous birds. Though flightless, his kick could be fatal. Let's face it, he was a walking feathered catastrophe. A most perilous character.

His former position as Chief Technical Officer of the Advanced Super Computing Center UUI, afforded him an outstanding opportunity to exercise his formidable genius in the pursuit of cosmic superiority by exploiting highly sophisticated technology. He had major plans to capitalize on it. They failed!

We believe his albeit temporary exile on Gaea was the result of his then assistant, Byzantia Bonobo meeting a chimp named Joel at an astrophysics conference. They had danced around the concept of Multiverse travel until he fessed up and admitted he was from a different world. Joel was an Adept and could transit between worlds at will.

She talked him into taking her with him on his next trip. It was then she discovered that she too was an Adept. She also discovered that Homo Sapiens still existed. There on Gaea! That was a real shock. Joel had used up his allotted "Earth Time" on the last trip and stayed on at Gaea. Byzz returned to Earth but thought seriously about permanent planetary emigration.

When she returned to Earth and the Hexagon, in a moment of weakness, she shared her secret with Caleb. It was a big mistake and unfortunately, irretrievable. He pressured her into accompanying her to Gaea. He was not an Adept – just a "Passive" – and required the services of an Adept or the use of a transmission device to make the journey.

In typical Caleb fashion, while on Gaea, he stole a small portable transit device and brought it back to Earth. It sat ready for his use in a nondescript alcove near the server farm on the third floor of the Hexagon. It would get lots of use with his designs for interplanetary conquest.

As might be expected, the former CTO was not content with traveling to one world. He was convinced there were many just waiting for him to conquer. He no longer needed Byzz to transit. He had the device and used it. Delusions of cosmic grandeur overcame his common sense and he began experimenting in earnest. His efforts often resulted in near disaster but he was not deterred.

Octavius Bear and that ridiculous Porcupine Howard Watt would no longer have a corner on Multiverse travel. As in all things technological and otherwise, they would have to contend with Caleb Cassowary. He set out to totally destroy the Bear's Empire through ransomware extortion. He botched it and brought international wrath down upon his wattled head. He and Byzz escaped though, using Quantum Motion to land and hide on Gaea.

But he persisted in his plans of cosmic domination. The galaxy would have lived in awe of him. No, not just one galaxy. His aspirations were intergalactic and beyond. In fact, his idol, Imperius Drake, was a piker. He only wanted world domination. Caleb looked far beyond that. The Multiverse! Gaea would be his first major target. He itched to kick out at Homo Sapiens. They once dominated the Earth and now Gaea. He would show them true dominance. He'd knock them into shape and then bury them with his startling intelligence. Then, with an army of interplanetary minions he would go on to conquer one sphere after another, including, of course, Earth.

*****

But first, Biosphere X –The Home World. He planned to cripple Earth then on to Gaea from the bird exoplanet. They had sparred with the Octavians, General Turmoil's agency, The Business, and suffered serious losses. Caleb would have seen that didn't happen again. Avians were superior and he was the supreme Avian. Of course, now he's dead – the remains of his body floating through space. But what about those crazy birds?

The Protector *(Dictator)* of the Home World had named Caleb his Chancellor, a new title in the realm. Some members of the Council were dubious but they all went along with the Protector's wishes. (*as usual*) A Falcon, Peregrine, the youngest Council member, had taken up the responsibilities of readying the Home World for Cyber War under Caleb's direction. But where was the Chancellor? He had gone to Gaea but had not been heard from for the past week.

Peregrine broached the subject at the Council meeting. No one, including the Protector could shed any light on the subject. The Army's Generalissimo, who had rapidly developed a hatred of the Cassowary after he had recommended that the military commander be fired was first to remark on his absence.

"He has disappeared, Lord Protector. That bird is a fake with all his vaunted technology expertise. He is going to subject us to another humiliating defeat."

The Protector squawked, "It is your responsibility to ensure that doesn't happen, General! Meanwhile, Young Peregrine, find my

Chancellor. We must prepare for the destruction of Earth. I shall be revenged on that execrable Horse and that abominable Bear. The Chancellor made me a sacred promise."

"I believe he is on Gaea, My Lord. We will initiate a search."

"See to it! And you Generalissimo, I will not tolerate another failure. You and your staff are flying on borrowed time."

The Hawk bowed his head but vowed his own personal revenge both on the Chancellor and on Councilor Peregrine, that sniveling Falcon.

The Falcon turned to the General. "Generalissimo. I have a requirement. We must have five volunteers to carry out the role of hackers in our upcoming cyberattack. They must be technically skilled, highly disciplined and unquestionably loyal to Home World and The Protector. It is they who will bring our vengeance to that cursed planet."

"They will report to my new associate, sent from Gaea by the Chancellor. He is a Great Horned Owl named Mattingly and he is fierce, unbelievably clever and highly skilled technically. He will train your troops as he prepares the hardware and software needed for our great Cyber War."

The Generalissimo was livid with rage. "Lord Protector, I object. The Army has very few Information Technology specialists and I cannot spare five of my best avians to support this crackpot scheme."

The Protector stared at him with a highly malevolent gaze. "He shrieked, "Do it…NOW. Or else."

The General knew all too well what "or else" meant. The Protector and Council held him responsible for the failure of Home World to resist the Earth's attack. He was quite literally, "flying on borrowed time."

He bowed once again and stalked from the room, cursing Caleb, Peregrine and The Protector under his breath.

The Late CALEB CASSOWARY

Chapter Four

The team holds a meeting on Zoom.
There's an overall feeling of gloom.
They all feel insecure
And Belinda is sure
Nutty birds are now plotting their doom.

Belinda was apprehensive. With that hate-filled Cassowary out of the way, she should have been feeling safe. But she wasn't. It was clear he loathed Octavius and was only too eager to bring about death and destruction to the world at large in order to establish his supremacy. Before he tried to destroy Earth's GPS capability, had he also developed other attack plans with more planets? She was worried about Octavius, the Cubs, the Octavians and for that matter, all of civilization. Were UUI, the Hexagon, the Bear's Lair and Polar Paradise still safe?

"Tavi, what are we doing to protect ourselves?"

"We're on it, Bel. We've narrowed the threat down to Biosphere X."

"Biosphere X? That's the Home World of those insanely belligerent birds. They tried to fire bomb UUI and the Lair. They're worse than Caleb!"

"General Turmoil's attack on them in retribution for their assaults here has toned them down a good deal. He killed off the Protector *(Their Leader)* and the entire governing Council. He did quite a bit of physical damage in the process. The new leaders will think twice before staging another attack. I need to get back to the Horse."

"But they must be boiling over with thoughts of revenge. Caleb was insane enough to feed that rage. Did he get them stirred up? Sorry, I don't share your confidence."

"I'm not confident. But we have an action plan and we're about to implement it."

"Let me help."

"We'll be using everyone except the Cubs! Where are they, by the way?"

*****

(Down in the technology bowels of the mansion)

Arabella jumped up from her terminal.

"Hi Momma and Poppa! We're working on the next version of The Bold Brave Brilliant Bumptious Bears game. It's almost ready for beta test. Wanna see?"

"We have a whole new cast of characters. Uncle Bruce is in it. *(The Great Detective).* So are Uncle Davey, *(The Duke)* Dancing Dan *(The Boxer)* and Flame! She's a talking fire engine. They're the Fire Squad."

"Uncle Preston has a sub program all his own. He's a world famous hero. We call him the Polar Potentate. You two are in it, too. *(The Rich Bears who are the parents of The Bold Brave Brilliant Bumptious Bears. That's us.)*"

McTavish interrupted, "Aunt Chita and Otto have been characters for a while now but we've updated them with new talents. Otto not only 'zaps,' he flies, and Aunt Chita can be invisible, except sometimes she leaves a spot or two behind like that Cheshire cat. Uncle Maury's one of the originals."

"We finally got the Frau and Colonel to agree to play. We call them the Wily Wolves. Uncle Howard and Marlin don't want to join in but we're still working on them. The Flying Tigers are naturals. A brother and sister who pilot planes, helicopters and rockets around the world. We keep them very busy."

"We just started on Huntley Husky. He's going to be a ghost dog – Hauntley – all grey with his blue eyes and bushy tail."

"Poppa, can we include the Prince of Whales and his dolphins? He'd be terrific!"

"Absolutely NOT! Someday, he'll be the King. No royalty!"

"Aww Gee! Anyway, we have too many heroes and not enough bad guys. Can we use Caleb and those crazy birds on Home World?"

Belinda winced. "No you can't. They're a serious problem. Not for games. Come up with some imaginary villains. "you're good at it."

"Maybe we'll bring Imperius Drake and Bigg back from the dead."

Octavius grinned, "That might work. Make sure to make them very ugly."

The Bearoness snorted. 'They were ugly without needing any special effects. How many characters do you two have in this game?"

"Sixty! We're trying for a hundred in the next version."

"How do you keep track of them all?"

"We don't. Uncle Condo has loaned us a couple of his staff members who love games and they are managing the infrastructure *(is that a word?)* for us."

"I'm not sure I like the idea of Hexagon personnel working on your games when they should be engaged in other work."

"But, Poppa, think of the money the game is bringing in for us. It's more profitable than a lot of the Advanced Center's other projects."

Belinda stifled a laugh and Octavius just snorted.

Chapter Five

It's a building that's really complex.
I refer to the UUI Hex.
Senhor Condo's in charge.
It's incredibly large.
And it's built to Octavian specs.

Ta-Da!! The Advanced Super Computing Center of UUI in the Kentucky hills. Until recently the exclusive domain of Caleb Cassowary, whose body is now floating somewhere in Quantum Space. Senhor L. Condor, *(Condo)* Brazilian communications and computing virtuoso has taken charge of the facility. It is an awesome place and he is an awesome genius. Another bird but vastly different from crazy Caleb or those nuts on Home World.

Envision a mile-square, four story, six sided, copper colored structure capped with antennas, a helipad and solar panel arrays and surrounded by wind turbines and parking lots. The bottom two stories are taken up with utilities and power supplies feeding the insatiable demands of the main frames, servers and quantum computing units that completely occupy the third floor. The top floor is mostly open plan with work and gathering spaces where designers, developers, programmers, coders, data analysts, cloud and artificial intelligence support teams ply their respective trades. The Pentagon on steroids. Tucked away in one wing is a column of offices assigned to the Hex management brain trust. Condo has taken over Caleb's offices.

He is sitting in front of a large screen in a Zoom session with Howard Watt, Marlin, Octavius, Colonel Wyatt Where, the Frau, Belinda and me. Ursula 12 occupies one panel of the display. The Octavians on parade!

As usual, Octavius has taken the lead. "Greetings, all. Time for a brief skull session and report. Settling in, Condo?"

"We're making good progress, Octavius. This place can be overwhelming. The staff is superb. Now that Byzz is back, the Ursula program is running at full speed. Caleb had a winner with her."

I laughed, "But then he ran roughshod over her."

"True, Maury, hatred of him was practically universal but most of the staff stayed on because they are immersed in spectacular projects with a pack of geniuses. Of course, Octavius, you've been paying them very well."

"It helps. We still have quite a mess to clean up and the business demands are accelerating in spite of the recent wreckage by Caleb."

"We're coping nicely. The satellites are back online. Thank goodness, Byzz got Caleb before he destroyed GPS. We believe it's stable. We're working with the US Space Force to check it all out. The Cloud is flourishing. Deep Data analysis is on the rise."

"There are also several mergers and acquisitions waiting in the wings. I gather these suitors and suitees feel a lot more comfortable with us now that the Cassowary has departed."

The Dolphin splashed affirmation. "But now we may have Biosphere X to contend with. Any thoughts, Ursula?"

As usual, the AGI was taking all this in, analyzing and measuring as she went.

"They could be a threat, Marlin. You should contact General Turmoil, Doctor Bear."

"That's my next call. We need to also bear in mind that Caleb was running around with an immense amount of Top-Secret and Beyond material in that grotesque head of his. That threat is over. I don't know what clearances Byzz has."

Condo replied. "Not sure! You should also know developing Ursula 13 is high on my priority list."

The Colonel commented. "We need to inform law enforcement that Caleb is dead. I suggest we report it as an accident. We don't want Byzz being prosecuted and we can't convince many of the cops that alternate worlds exist. We need to get Bruce's advice on that one."

I raised a paw. "You said a magic word, Wyatt. Bruce Wallaroo. Where is he?"

Octavius replied. "On his way here. As you know, Interpol reassigned him to work on this case. He went back to Lyon for some meetings but he'll be flying in shortly. He'll want to be in on the wrap up. So will Agent Badger of the FBI. She believes in the Multiverse."

Ursula chimed in *(literally)* "You know, I'm glad we're including Otto and the Frau in this session. They have major contributions to make. Otto has become our premiere quantum traveler and the Frau is just incredible. Now that the Butler is on board, she has fewer domestic issues to worry about. By the way, how is he working out?"

"Huntley? He seems to be adapting very nicely. Belinda and the Frau are both pleased, aren't you, Ladies? *(They both smiled and nodded.)* They've been turning over more and more assignments to him. I like him. The Cubs like him. They want him in their game. They call him Hauntley, the Ghost Husky. What do you think of him, Maury?"

I was still fence sitting. "So far, so good!"

Howard and Marlin approved of him. Condo had moved out of the mansion and taken rooms near the Hexagon so he had no opinion. The Colonel was noticeably quiet. A handsome Husky around the Frau may not have been sitting all that well with him. A little jealousy perhaps? We shall see.

The Bear turned to Howard. "Is it time for a little Biosphere X reconnaissance? What's your confidence level that they're up to something?"

"Pretty high but we can't be sure until we actually look.

"Sounds like another spy job for Otto. He loves this stuff. See if you can get him up on the screen. He's standing by."

The Zoom screen shifted and a goofy face came up in a new panel. Otto was staring into his laptop. "You rang?"

"Yes, your Magnificence. We have need of your wonderful skills."

"I live to serve. What ridiculous assignment have you prepared for me this time, Maury?"

"Biosphere X!"

"Ah, Biosphere X. – The Home World! Many an evening I have spent being chased around that rotten exoplanet. Just once can I go someplace nice?"

"Next time. I promise. Howard and Marlin have the specs for this trip. Bring an Ursula with you, of course."

"Of course! Home World! What do I do when I get there?"

"Nose around. Establish contacts. See if they're preparing for war. Especially cyberwar. If need be, we'll come and support you. Have Ursula call us. Remember, they can be killers. Be your unobtrusive self."

"I am a paragon of unobtrusivity – is that a word?"

"No!"

"OK, General Turmoil wiped out all of the last Council and the Protector with his retaliatory raids. I suppose there's a new cast of characters."

"Yes, and we think they're worse than their predecessors. We also believe Caleb got them stirred up about revenge against Earth, especially the General and Octavius. At least, that's what Byzz assumed from his rantings before she did him in."

"Oh swell! Nothing like a little rampaging to spice up the situation. You know, Maury and Octavius, I enjoy this interplanetary 'zapping' but I also have developed a fondness for my flat, fat tail. Ursula's a great help but this time, I'm going to pack a few weapons. I assume you have no objection to a little self-defense."

The Great Bear roared. "Absolutely! Take an entire arsenal with you and don't hesitate to use it. We'll have Howard, the Colonel and Frau on standby to back you up, if you need them. The problem has always been that you're the only Octavian who can 'zap.' The Frau can move at hyperspeed but she has limited range. Chita's fast too but she won't do quantum travel."

"Yeah, I know! That damn Duck and his serum set me up as a flying freak. It's fun sometimes but one of these days, I'm going to get stuck. What kind of shape are their military and police in?"

"I doubt if they've recovered but it's pretty certain that if Caleb was engineering their vengeance ventures, it will be cyberwar. They tried physical attacks and failed miserably. We don't know how far the Cassowary advanced them with malware and attack hardware before the Bonobo blasted him off that GPS satellite. We also don't know who, if anybody, is capable of carrying on for Caleb. We're not sure they know he's dead and we don't want to enlighten them. Keep that in mind!"

"Gotcha! OK, Howard, Ursula, Marlin, Colonel, Ilse. Let's go - Space, the Final Frontier!"

Chapter Six

Now Caleb was clearly absurd.
No, 'deadly" is really the word.
But Condo instead
Just keeps plugging ahead.
He's quite a remarkable bird.

Maury here. Let us briefly return to The Advanced Super Computing Center of UUI - the Hexagon - and consider once again Senhor L. Condor, *(Condo)* newly appointed CTO of the complex.

Condo is an Andean Condor, *Vultur Gryphus,* a native of the South American wilds. He came in from the mountains and established himself in Sao Paolo, one of the world's largest cities, to pursue his passion for telecommunications. It started out as compensation for the fact that Andean Condors have no voice box and can't make any kind of vocal sound. *(See Book 2 – The Case of the Spotted Band.)* The Condor has since remedied that through the wonders of microchip technology and avian biology. Today, courtesy of a highly miniaturized, embedded vocal device, he can create any sound and often entertains by imitating the voices of his audience.

Bruce Wallaroo has known Condo for quite a while. I first met him when Bruce and I were on the run from a Brazilian gangster named Pontius Puma. Condo used his impressive network equipment and phenomenal technical knowledge to totally destroy the Puma's criminal infrastructure.

We exited Sao Paolo with three of the four members of the Spotted Band who were also on Pontius Puma's hit list. Chita *(his mate at the time)* was the fourth member but had taken off separately. This was before she joined the good guys and ended up as a card carrying Octavian.

Belinda took the Aquabear SST to Sao Paolo on a rescue mission and after some neat work finessing customs and border police flew the six of us back to Cincinnati.

With the Puma seeking revenge, the Condor decided things were too hot for him in Brazil and since he had shut down his personal tech center before leaving, he decided to stay with us at the Bear's Lair. We caught the Puma trying to attack us and he is serving a long jail sentence. But Condo hung on for a "short while."

A short while became a long while and Condo has settled in with us and has participated in a number of wild adventures that I have recorded in the many volumes of the Casebooks. He is now an active and essential Octavian.

As I said, he is a technical genius. Certainly on a par and probably more advanced than Caleb Cassowary. When that dirty bird staged his extortion try and failed, he and his assistant Byzz headed for the hills. That is, another planet courtesy of the wonders of Multiverse travel. That left a gap at the top of the Hexagon and Octavius called on Condo to fill it.

He is doing exceptionally well in command of the Advanced Center.

It didn't take very long for the Center staff to rally around him and after picking up the pieces caused by Caleb's blitz, they have UUI's global telecom and computing offerings on an even keel and advancing admirably. The Cloud and Deep Data Analytics businesses are going gangbusters.

A piece of the puzzle still not firmly in place is the Ursula advancement program. These robotic marvels have served us brilliantly to the point that we cannot function without them. The program was under the direction of Byzz. She is now back at the Hex and working on the development of Ursula 13. She had also been the CTO's aide but is no longer in that position. The Condor is not comfortable with the idea of her as his assistant.

At the moment, in addition to her ubiquitous support throughout the Octavian universe, Ursula 12 is filling in as Condo's deputy but a red panda named Li-Ping is being groomed for the job.

The Hex is known and respected worldwide for the high quality and sophisticated technology processes and products it generates. Caleb for all his crazy faults, did manage to produce some wonderful stuff under his regime. Perhaps I should say the Hex managed to produce some wonderful stuff in spite of Caleb. Who knows? Byzantia certainly despised him to the point of killing him and rescuing the GPS system from total oblivion.

Now, the Condor has managed to put the Center into the forefront of advanced civilian and military development rivaling the Business and General Turmoil. Both enterprises will be front and center in the conflict that's brewing with the paranoid birds. It's a touchy relationship, at best.

Add to this, the Multiverse Project under Howard's direction which has potential conflicts with the alternative universe activities of the Business and you have a truly Byzantine Cosmic situation. Oh well, it makes life interesting as that old-time Chinese saying goes.

Anyway, you will be hearing much more about Condo and his fantastic abilities as our story progresses. Stand by.

Meanwhile…

Chapter Seven

They have never quite gotten along.
Each one thinks that the other is wrong.
The Great Bear says, "It's so!"
To the General's "No!"
Yes, their rivalry's really quite strong.

"I guess there's nothing for it. I'll have to call General Turmoil and give him an update on Caleb's demise and our concerns about Biosphere X. He probably knows already but just in case. Then when Bruce arrives, we can take up how we explain Caleb's death to Earth law enforcement."

The Great Bear shrugged and asked me to set up a Zoom session with Old Crazy Horse. That was never an easy process. The Business is very protective. In fact, they seldom admit they even exist. They operate in a shadowy but aggressive world of deception and intrigue and none is more deceptive and "intriguish" than the Director, General Turmoil. He and Octavius have been both enemies and allies in the past. Neither trusts the other but sometimes necessity makes for strained cooperation.

Such was the case with the paranoid birds of Biosphere X. They staged an attack on a seminar at MIT dealing with Quantum Motion and the Multiverse. Convinced that Earth was going to attack them, they sought to kill off the participants most likely to make that happen. They failed but just bearly.

The General, incensed at the onslaught, staged a massive counterattack on the exoplanet and wiped out much of their offensive and defensive capability, killing off the Protector and all the member of the Council. Two Homeworld operatives still on Earth after they had bungled the MIT strike, staged a futile attempt at firebombing Octavius' Bear's Lair and UUI in retribution for the destruction and mayhem wreaked upon the exoplanet. They perished in a fiery cataclysm caused by an Ursula.

Since that time, the Home World had been quiescent as they set about reconstructing their government and their armaments. That is, until Caleb Cassowary arrived and reignited their lust for revenge on Earth and desires to rule the universe. Caleb perished at the paws of Byzantia, his one-time assistant, while attempting to destroy Earth's GPS capabilities. He is gone but his agitation for vengeance lingers on.

That's the message Octavius is about to share with the General.

We went through the usual availability nonsense and once more the Great Bear had to identify himself clearly in order to get an officious underling to summon the General. Finally, the face of a black horse appeared on the screen.

"Hello, Doctor Bear, we have to stop meeting like this. I assume you have news of our feathered fiend."

Octavius chuckled and said, "I have good news and I have bad news. First, the good. Our ex-feathered fiend, Caleb Cassowary is no more or did you already know that?"

Genuine surprise on the horse's face. "Did you kill him?"

"Not our style, General. He was done in by his assistant – Byzantia Bonobo while he was attempting to destroy Earth's GPS network. He had the knowledge, skills and wherewithal to do it, too. His shattered remains are floating somewhere in nearby space. We're debating whether to try to recover the body."

"Not a bad idea. It would be proof positive that he's dead."

"Byzz insists that he was torn apart by a heavy duty laser that she personally fired. We believe her. We don't expect charges to be placed against her by either Interpol or the FBI. Some of my staff want to declare her a heroine. She's back working for us. *(No mention of the Ursula program. The General definitely did not have a need to know.)* It was a near miss for Earth's PNT systems. *(Positioning, Navigation, and Timing)* That could have brought our world to its knees."

"We're well aware of the fragility and vulnerability of GPS. The government is working on backups and work arounds but we're not there yet. This event may speed things up in certain circles. Anyway, thank the Bonobo for me. She can work for us any time if she wants to."

"I think we'll keep her."

"I thought so. Now, what's your bad news?"

"We believe Biosphere X is at it again. Caleb got them stirred up for world conquest. At least, that's what he told the Bonobo."

"They'll never learn. I thought we had them subdued for a good long while. Can they do anything without the Cassowary?"

"That's what we intend to find out. I don't believe they're going to do any more firebombing. Caleb was promoting cyber warfare. We're going to send out a scouting mission. One of my elusive crew who's been there before and knows a bit about hacking and denial of service."

"I may send someone, too. *(He already had. Mattingly the Owl.)* I'll let you know. I don't share your reluctance to use lethal force, as you're well aware. Those birds are a scourge. We ought to wipe out the entire planet."

"Some of my team share your opinion."

"Well, Doctor Bear. Please keep me posted and I'll do the same. Their military is definitely sclerotic and technologically passé but we can't become overconfident. Their new Protector is a real fanatic on avian superiority. He and Caleb must have been quite a pair. I wonder who's going to run their war program now."

"That's one thing we aim to find out. If they have a program."

"Oh, I bet they do!"

"That's a wager I won't touch. Good-bye, General! Talk to you again."

We signed off.

The Great Bear sat musing. "The General was too calm and smooth about all this. I'm sure I didn't tell him anything he didn't already know. As we speak, he probably has an agent on Home World working away on undermining anything Caleb had in the works. I'm not going to take him on if he wants to do all the grunt work."

"But I don't want to destroy the Home World, tempting though it may be. There's a massive population of innocent birds who have been victimized by their despotic leaders for far too long. The regime has to fall but Biosphere X has to survive. I doubt if the General sees it that way."

Octavius turned to me. "Get Otto, Howard, Marlin, the Frau and the Colonel. Call up Condo. Tell him to get Byzz and join us on Zoom. We have some strategizing to do before Otto leaves for the Home World. Damn those birds."

Here we go again.

Chapter Eight

The Home World or Biosphere X
Is controlled by a buzzard called Rex.
They intend to fight back
For a past Earth attack.
It's a planet that's covered with wrecks.

(Biosphere X - In the Audience Chamber of the Protector)

Councilor Peregrine approached the Protector's perch and waited to be recognized.

Rex, the Protector, a very large, grizzled Buzzard, was now the exoplanet Dictator and was entrusted by The Supreme Council with assuring the existence of Biosphere X *(known to them as Home World)* remained a closely guarded secret. The Home World Councilors, all of them some species of Raptor, were aware of alternate universes and expended major efforts, motivated by paranoia, to prevent exposure while they in turn, examined the Multiverse for threats and opportunities for conquest.

A special team of avian voyagers had arrived on Earth fourteen years ago and had subtly inserted themselves into environments from which they could observe and report any possible efforts to uncover Home World's existence. They were authorized to take radical steps as necessary, to discourage or abort any such efforts.

After years of inaction, they discovered an experimental platform on Earth to remotely affect electrons in other universes. Octavius Bear's Multiverse program. Home World was a target environment. This could not be allowed to proceed or, worse yet, succeed. Two of the team, a Shrike and a Cormorant, were appointed to sabotage the effort. They failed.

The Protector looked up.

"Yes, Peregrine. What is it? Have you found the Chancellor?"

"No, Your Worship. We have searched here, on Gaea and even on Earth. We have reason to believe that he recently transported to Gaea from the Homeworld after leaving your presence but we can't find him although I have had messages from him. Our investigators think he may gone into protective hiding while he negotiates with Gaean conspirators."

"Earlier on, he left Earth in haste for Gaea with his Bonobo assistant under a serious cloud of suspicion of wrongdoing. She remained on Gaea while he proceeded here to our sacred Homeworld. She can no longer be found either They are probably both in hiding to avoid being captured by Earthlings."

The Protector frowned. "That just confirms my suspicions that Earth is planning yet another attack on us. Our physical defenses are still in a weakened state from that abominable Horse's attacks and between the two of us, our military is next to worthless. The Chancellor was correct. We must rely on technology and conduct all out cyber warfare. In his absence, I need a strong, knowledgeable and ruthless leader here to carry it off. As far as cyber terrorism is concerned, the Generalissimo and his staff are as naïve as chicks in the nest. Are you up to the challenge?"

"Indeed, I am, Lord Protector. The Chancellor left instructions and I have been expanding and improving on them. As I told you, I have also found a technically skilled assistant to make our program a reality. I have the Army volunteers. It will take a little time and some expense to build our resources but we will have a cyber assault capability second to none when we have completed our work."

"How much time and how much expense?"

"I will have a plan for you and the Council in two moon's time."

"Very well! See to it!"

The Peregrine strutted out and then flew to the converted warehouse where his crack team awaited his further instructions. Also there stood a newcomer. A Great Horned Owl – Mattingly by name –

who had arrived two days ago claiming he had been sent by Chancellor Caleb to move the project along while the Cassowary negotiated hardware, software and network facilities from his sources on Gaea. He showed the Falcon a series of texts from Caleb outlining his bona fides and strong technical capabilities. Peregrine fell for it. *(Caleb, of course, was now floating lifeless among the satellites.)*

Actually, Mattingly was a freelance cyber mercenary employed by General Turmoil and charged with sabotaging the Home World's planned cyberwar. Not merely sabotage. He was to install malware that would wreak destruction on Biosphere X when they attempted to launch their attack. Hopefully the Protector and Council would be victims. Project Boomerang!

Chapter Nine

Otto's up for a Multiverse Trip.
Through the cosmos he'll rapidly zip.
His excursion is slick.
Quantum motion's the trick
And he's doing it without a ship.

(The Bear's Lair - Bearonial Suite)

An Octavian Zoom and Skull session had just begun in anticipation of Otto's departure to Biosphere X. The Great Bear, Otto, Howard, Marlin, Belinda, Chita, the Frau, Colonel and I were there in person at the Lair. Condo and Byzz were on the oversize screen as was the ubiquitous Ursula 12. A new face had joined them. A Red Panda from the Himalayas named Li-Ping. He had just been named as Condo's new assistant. More about him shortly.

Chief Inspector Bruce Wallaroo had not yet arrived. As usual, Octavius took charge.

"OK, folks, it's follow-up time. Thanks to Byzz, we no longer have Caleb Cassowary alive and doing his thing BUT we don't know what he left behind. I'm concerned that he has set off a cyber terrorism and cyber warfare capability on Biosphere X and maybe on Gaea, as well. You saw him last, Byzz. What's your take?"

"First off, Doctor Bear I want to thank you and Senhor Condor for taking me back. Working for Caleb was a horror show. Megalomania to the nth degree! I'm delighted to be working on the Ursulas again. Number 12 is a prize but number 13 will be even more sensational. Sorry, Ursie!"

The AGI rang her chime in acknowledgement.

"As for Caleb stirring things up on the Home World, I'm positive he did. They were a key part of his intergalactic power play. They do not have much in the way of advanced computer and communications technology but Caleb had designed an elaborate upgrade program. What he wanted from them was their extreme fanaticism – "avians über alles." A feathered mob that he could mold. Birds that were obsessed with seeing enemies on every planet. Paranoids. He bragged about how Biosphere X would become Cyber Warfare Central."

Belinda interrupted, "But he's no longer there. Is there someone who can carry on his nefarious plans?"

Byzz shrugged. "I'm not sure. Their military is useless but there are several members of the Supreme Council who seemed eager to work with Caleb. A young Falcon named Peregrine may be the new cyber war leader. He's a new member of the Council. I don't know anything about him. I just heard his name from Caleb."

Octavius thanked her. "Otto! Sorry about asking you to make another trip back to the Home World. We need to find out about this Councilor Peregrine and what the birds' plans are. Think you can stand another run?"

"Why not? It beats capering with the Aquabears. No offense, Bearoness."

"None taken, Otto. You're such a brave little fellow. I just wish more of us knew how to "zap" the way you do."

"I wish I knew how to "zap" the way I do. Well Howard and Marlin, let's get me prepped for another Multiverse Move."

The Colonel growled. "Take a laser weapon with you, Otto. Better yet, take two. Those nutty avians don't fool around. And of, course take an Ursula."

Ursula 12 chuckled. "He's not going anywhere without me."

Condo interrupted. "Otto, come on over to the Hexagon before you leave. We'll give you a crash course on cyber warfare techniques.

That will help you interpret what they're doing, if anything. You too, Ursula."

Octavius said, "Maury, Chita, Colonel and Frau Ilse. You go too. I'm waiting for Bruce Wallaroo to arrive or I'd join you. How about you, Belinda? *(The Bearoness, for all her show biz and aristocratic background was no technical slouch. After all, she piloted the Octavian Air Force.)*

"Yes, I will. For once I can "out-technology" the Cubs. Can you imagine them as cyber terrorists? I'd lock them up forever."

"No, but they might make good cyber cops. Anyway, let's keep them out of this."

"Thank goodness they're all tied up with their Internet game. If they knew what we are about, they'd be all over us. Octavius, who is this Li-Ping we saw with Condo and Byzz?"

"He's a red panda from the Himalayas. Why they call themselves pandas, I don't know. As you saw, he's small with golden fur, white face and ears and a big striped tail They look nothing like those big black and white roley-poleys. Remember Jane Huang Hau? She's a panda."

"The cinematographer? How could I forget. She pushed that polar ingenue off a balcony at the Castle." *(See Book 10 – The Camera Case)*

"True, but her lawyer got her off with a plea of self-defense. She's back working for Preston. Anyway, this Li-Ping is, like many Asiatic animals, a technology whiz-kid. He has been working at the Hex for several years, mostly in Deep Data Analytics and Quantum Computing. He's been supporting Jaguar Jack and his horse racing package. Still does. Since Condo is a telecommunications expert, their backgrounds complement each other's. Byzz recommended him. He's a bit of a nocturnal type. Liked the night shift but he jumped at the chance to work bedside the CTO. We'll see how it turns out."

"Well, Condo could certainly use the help. He's working around the clock. Caleb left quite a mess but the Condor is doing a great job getting things under control."

"He's a gem. How many cases has he assisted in? He's a dyed in the wool Octavian. I'm delighted Bruce Wallaroo introduced him to us."

And now, on cue! A UUI whirlybird thrummed its way toward the Bear's Lair helipad. In addition to the Octavian Air Force at the Bear's Lair, UUI sported a fleet of helicopters ranging from small runabouts to huge utility ships. Chief Inspector Bruce Wallaroo of Interpol was arriving on one of their shuttles.

Octavius and Bel rose from their chairs and sauntered out to form a welcoming committee.

Maury Meerkat

Chapter Ten

The species that's called Wallaroo
Is a wallaby plus kangaroo.
His large feet - (macropod!)
Make him look rather odd.
But I bet he moves faster than you.

Maury here once again. When the Cassowary Caper first blew up, Interpol assigned a good friend of mine, Chief Inspector Bruce Wallaroo to the case based on his long association with Octavius Bear. Currently on assignment from Australia to Interpol in Lyon, France, Bruce snagged a commercial flight to New York and switched to one of UUI's shuttle helicopters for the run to the Bear's Lair. Some public and legal relations clean-up after Caleb's demise was necessary.

The sound of thumping rotors thundered over the grounds of the Bear's Lair. The UUI chopper hovered over the massive courtyard and settled gracefully onto the helipad. The Great Bear loped out of the mansion with the Butler Huntley Husky in tow. Belinda joined them. The copter's cargo door opened and two oversized marsupial feet stomped impatiently. Chief Inspector Bruce Wallaroo of Interpol had arrived. Octavius held out his giant paws in greeting.

"Good to see you again, Bruce. Watch the rotors. Huntley here has some cold beers ready for you. How was the trip?"

"The plane ride was fine, Ocko. G'day Bearoness. Great to see you again. Beautiful as usual. Any road, next time I'm going to stay over in New York. Haven't been there in a while. As for helicopters, as you know, we have a great history. I love the flying Mix Masters. *(See Book One – The Open and Shut Case. Another story for another time.)*

"C'mon in. Thanks for making the journey. We need to get our stories straight on what happened to Caleb so we can pass it on to the law enforcement community and the press. A little legal authority from you and Special Agent Badger will help a lot. We don't want to tell the true story of how close we came to losing GPS except to government types with a need to know."

Belinda said, "I'm heading out to the Hex for a briefing. As you might expect, the twins have been asking for you all day. And say hello to our new Butler, Huntley Husky."

"Good on 'em. Be lovely to see them again. He reached out and shook Huntley's paw. "Nice to meet you. Do you have idea what you signed up for? Run while you still have a chance."

Laughs all around.

He hopped into the Ursine Lounge. "G'day all! Grand to see you. G'day Maury! G'day Chita! Hey, Otto! Colonel! Howard, Marlin!!" They were all getting a last drink in before parting for the Hex.

The Frau as usual had disappeared. The Inspector with his furniture wrecking bouncing and jumping was the bane of her existence. Huntley, the Butler watched the Inspector spring off a table and into a chair. He was taken aback.

Before a sensible conversation could start, two whirlwinds descended on the lounge. "Uncle Bruce! Hi, Uncle Bruce! C'mon! You can help us with our Bumptious Game." They tugged on his arms and accidentally tromped on his super-size feet.

"Ouch! Hey, young ones. You're getting too big for jumping around." *(Talk about pots calling kettles black.)* I'll come by in a little while. I have some serious legal business to discuss with your Momma and Poppa and your Aunts and Uncles."

Mlle Woof, with great effort, shooed the Furballs out of the Lounge.

Bruce settled in, can of Foster's in his paw and asked, "Are we sure Caleb's remains are truly floating about in space?"

"Actually, we only have Byzantia's word for it. But I trust her. She's back at the Hex working on developing Ursula 13."

"Alright, we've already decided not to prosecute her. I assume she will keep her mouth shut. She's not going to brag about saving the world, is she?"

"I'll make sure she gets the message once again loud and clear."

"OK, so let's do some damage control. He's dead. No mention of space, alternate worlds and GPS satellites. He died on Earth and his body can't be recovered. We need a couple of reliable witnesses to attest to that. How did he die?"

The Colonel looked over. "How about an over-water air crash. Could he fly a plane?"

Nobody knew. But it was rejected because it would have involved an air safety investigation.

"I don't suppose we could use an accident over a waterfall."

"Nah! That's been done over and over again."

"How about he was accidentally atomized while trying to explode a bomb at the Hexagon? That would play to his character."

"That might work. Chita, you're good at fiction. Can you create the story? Hexagon security will have to be briefed. I doubt that will be a problem. They all hated Caleb and I'm sure they'll be more than willing to support the report. I think we need to give Agent Badger the straight skinny. She's aware of space travel and Caleb's abilities. She knows he was off planet."

Octavius looked up at the ceiling. "Otto, I feel a bit guilty sending you off on yet another Multiverse run. This one could be dangerous. However you're a natural Adept and that telekinetic ability is a major plus. You're the only one of the Octavians who combines both of those talents."

The Otter grinned and said, "I know. I never thought I'd appreciate the treatments Imperius Drake was performing on me but it seems they're working out well. Ironic! He'd be totally disgusted to learn I'm using them for good. He wanted me to be a prototype of his Storm Troopers. Sorry! I'm just glad I didn't go insane as a result."

"Nope, you have a clean bill of health from Odd Vark and the UUI medics. Are you still checking in with them?"

"Oh, yeah! I have no desire to end up as a nut case. I'll keep showing up for my tests. So far, they're been really encouraging. Anyway, we have a date with Condo, Byzz and his staff to be briefed on cyber warfare techniques. Are we all heading for the Hex?"

The Octavians plus Belinda got up from their positions and headed out to the main courtyard where two large vans were standing by. Bruce decided to join them. A little cyberwar education never hurt. Since Bruce would be out of the mansion, the Frau's trepidation for the furniture faded and she came along. So did Octavius.

Huntley wagged his tail in salute. Off to the Kentucky hills and the Advanced Technology Center for a short course in cyber warfare. Then, in Otto and Ursula's case, off to Biosphere X and exercise in spying and "zapping."

On the trip over, Octavius briefed the Inspector on our surmises about the Home World. He wasn't surprised. "Those birds are born with a few screws loose. Are they all like that?"

The Great Bear replied. "That's one of the things we want to find out. If there's a group that's opposed to their hostility, we want to find them and hopefully, give them a boost. That's one of the things Otto here is set to discover."

"By the way, I should tell you that General Turmoil is probably involved. He didn't know about Caleb's demise but he did know the Cassowary was stirring something up on the Biosphere."

"Well, we get rid of one nut case and end up dealing with another. We haven't been able to convince the US government to disband that operation. They won't even admit it exists."

The Bear puffed out his cheeks. "In this case, it might be a plus. He has a lot more in the way of cyberwar technology smarts than I do and they have a development and manufacturing capability that's state of the art. The Hex is phenomenal but its mission is different. We're not in the warfare business, At least, not intentionally. Anyway, we'll just have to see how it all plays out. Otto and Ursula are a formidable pair."

Speaking of whom, as they rode along, Otto was being prepped by the AGI. "We need to find out all we can about this Peregrine character. Byzz didn't know that much about him except he was new on the scene, young and ambitious. He had a brief set of meetings with Caleb before the Cassowary took off for Gaea. I don't know how technically competent he is. I hope he's not. He'll be easier to fool if he thinks he knows more than he really does. Those birds in the Praesidium are not lacking in ego starting with the Protector."

The Otter shook his head. "That exoplanet is really stuck with a bunch of idiot leaders. Unfortunately, they're a bunch of dangerous idiots. I've heard there's an opposition party headed up by an Eagle. I don't know. He could be even worse. We'll just have to see."

The van came within sight of the Hexagon, the view of which always managed to kill conversation. Bruce was especially impressed. "Lord, Ocko, you certainly know how to spend money. The jackaroos in Canberra would sell their eyeteeth, if they had any, to work in a place like this."

"I want the folks here to be proud of themselves, of what they do and where they work."

"Well, if they're not, ship them out. What a spread."

Up to the copper colored doors.

The Development of Civilization-Volume 15
Part 3
<u>Some Brief Lessons in Cyberwarfare</u>
(From "An Introduction to Faunapology" by Octavius Bear Ph.D.)

What is Cyber Warfare? Definitions and alternate terms abound. Cyber War; Cyber Terrorism; Tech Attacks! One thing is common. The use of communications and computing technologies to damage the capabilities of a target entity. Most of these attacks are hardware and/or software based but physical assaults against infrastructures are not unknown. Electric grids, transport facilities, satellites and antennas, radio and television stations are just some examples of targets of physical destruction through bombing, fire, collision or riot.

The most common forms of Cyber Warfare involve denial of service, hacking, theft, file and software alteration or destruction, spoofing and undermining the applications that depend upon the technology. It is in the applications and data stores that extreme damage can be incurred. Imagine taking down an ATM system, a stock exchange, a hospital, an air or rail facility, GPS, water supply or a power grid for an extended period of time or perhaps even permanently. All done surreptitiously by an enemy without being identified or subjected to counter attack.

The advent of Cloud Computing with all of its efficiencies has nevertheless opened up an arena of vulnerability that can induce severe damage over a wide range of centralized users, systems ana applications.

Fundamental to all cyber-attacks is the ability to bypass access control mechanisms and intrusion detection. This is sometimes done directly but increasingly, rogue applications are invoked that evade detection by attaching themselves to legitimate processes and sneaking into the target environments. It is not uncommon for technology users to employ a wide variety of software sources. Their respective security measures may be incompatible or obsolete, thus exposing the overall structure.

New identification techniques such as fingerprint, voice, retina and dual passcodes are being utilized to reduce attacks by individuals but in the Internet of Things, many applications and devices communicate directly without human intervention. Therein lie major security vulnerabilities.

Denial of service is a sophisticated form of extortion as is ransomware. The victims are presented with the opportunities to stop the damage by paying for restoring the hostage files, programs and systems or in the case of transaction excess, stopping the incessant traffic overloading the network. In the case of Cyber War, however, the objective is malicious destruction. No payment desired.

The ability to decrypt hostile passwords is critical to defeating ransomware, assuming, of course that files, programs and systems have not been wantonly destroyed. Our Ursulas use their high speed circuits and Quantum Computing capabilities to make short work of the encryption employed by the attackers. We'll see how this works out shortly.

OTTO The Magnificent

Chapter Eleven

Otto's off to shut all those birds down.
While he may look to you like a clown,
He's a serious threat.
Bad guys shouldn't forget,
He's the smartest young otter in town.

After the Hexagon briefing, Otto returned to the Bear's Lair and the Multiverse Project rooms to prepare for his trip to Biosphere X. Packing his laser weapon and an Ursula 12 equipped laptop, he made ready for the journey. The Home World's atmosphere was breathable so he had no concern on that score. Of course, a backpack full of snacks and water were necessities.

He didn't plan to stay long – 48 hours at the most – enough time for him to poke around and size up the birds' technological abilities and intentions. He also wanted to find any pockets of resistance to the government, if they existed. Who was that rumored Eagle?

He had been to the biosphere before and knew about the intruder monitors that dotted the exoplanet's landscape. No doubt, they were still functioning even after the attacks by General Turmoil and his forces. His "zapping" abilities were going to be put to the test as he avoided being picked up by the sensors.

Unless they had improved dramatically, the Home World police and military were not much of a threat. But that's what he had to determine. He needed to track down this Council member – what's his name- Peregrine Falcon. According to Byzantia, Caleb in his guise as Chancellor had turned his Cyberwarfare plans over to him to execute. Did the Cassowary's disappearance scuttle the project? Something else for him to find out.

"OK, Howard! Ready when you are!"

Though he looked and often acted goofy, he was self-reliant, elusive and when necessary, deadly. As he had done in the past, he planned to telekinetically "zap" his way around the planetary landscape. But he relied on Howard and Marlin to do his initial targeting for him along with Ursula 12.

They handed him a galactic navigation device pre-loaded with coordinates. He is a Multiverse Adept and can quantum travel on his own power but he needed to know where he was going.

"We've spotted you near their capital but far enough away to evade detection. You are going to have some serious "zapping" to do to travel around. Good luck. We'll be standing by the whole time you're gone."

Octavius has trundled in, shook paws, thanked him and wished him well.

"And away we go!"

*****

A whooshing sound! Everything turning grey! Otto fell into the usual semi-consciousness that accompanies his quantum jumps. Seconds passed. Seemed like eternities. Then, that bump and thud as he hit the ground. He shook his head to clear the space induced cobwebs.

He looked around. The Homeworld sun was moving slowly toward the horizon casting shadows as it moved – correction, as the exoplanet moved. Biosphere X rotated rapidly around a Red Dwarf in the outer reaches of the Milky Way. Unlike our own Sun which is a somewhat brighter and hotter Yellow Dwarf.

Twittering sounds in the background. No surprise there. This was a bird's planet after all. He checked his backpack, navigator and the laptop containing a copy of Ursula 12.

"You OK, Ursie?"

She rang her chime. "My device is intact and my functions are all in order. As far as I can tell, we did not set off any of the Protector's intrusion monitors but I think we want to move along. We have company.'

He gazed up into the branches of a tree and found himself being stared at by a large and ominous Great Horned Owl.

Otto got ready to "zap." He stuttered "Who…Who?"."

The bird looked at him with his unblinking eyes. "That's my line, Sparky. Get yourself a new writer. Mattingly Owl, at your service. Matt to you. No need for telekinetics, my furry friend. I know you. We're on the same side."

Mattingly Owl

Ursula, not wanting to reveal herself to this unlikely bird, switched to passive mode - recording but not reacting, commenting or replying. Otto caught the change.

He looked up again at the Owl who was still staring with those unmoving, unblinking eyes and said, "And what side is that, if I may ask?"

"We've both been assigned to make sure these Home Worlders don't get electronically rambunctious. OK, I'll fess up. I'm an earth based technological freelancer currently employed by The Business. General Turmoil is one of my clients. A most generous client, I might add. He and your ursine boss don't always see eye to eye but this time, they do. He has a special place in his heart for this Biosphere crowd and it isn't affectionate. I've been commissioned to screw up their efforts at cyberwarfare. You may have noticed that I'm a Great Horned Owl – a fierce raptor, in fact. I fit right into this avian exoplanet whereas you, clever as you may be, are from the wrong species."

Otto chuckled. "I managed pretty well on my last trip here but I'll grant you that I had to keep appearing and disappearing. I call it "zapping.""

"A very useful and formidable talent, my furry friend. I have to rely on guile and wing power but I can move around and approach the powers-that-be without exciting too much attention. In fact, that's what I've already done."

"I've been here two days and I've negotiated a contract with this overly eager and naïve Falcon, Peregrine, to supply hacking and crypto hardware and software. I've shipped in a few faulty samples for his perusal. Samples supplied by the Business but he doesn't know that. He thinks they're coming from a clandestine outfit on Gaea that Caleb is doing business with."

"You know Caleb is dead?"

"Yes! Good riddance. A while back, he tried to enlist me in several of his 'conquer the universe' schemes. The guy was a nut. I don't suppose you'd like to tell me what or who brought about his demise."

"Not at the moment. It's important that these Home Worlders think he's still alive. The Chancellor is missing but still deemed viable."

"Gotcha, Sparky. Now let's get out of here and solidify our plans. Their Cyberwar program is chugging right along. This jerk Peregrine has managed to shanghai a set of tech warriors and I've been supplying hardware and software *(faulty, of course)* to support the process. Supposedly, we will use the networks on Gaea to launch the attacks. Would you be surprised if I told you, those links will not be functioning and the whole mess will backfire on their own infrastructure? Project Boomerang."

"Tricky name! How much wreckage will you cause?

"I believe the term is 'substantial.' They'll be picking up the pieces for quite a while."

"The General doesn't play around."

"And neither do I. I would not advise trying to stop me, if that's your intention."

"Never entered my mind!"

Chapter Twelve

It's that time for a business review.
Are the UUI profit claims true?
After Caleb's miscue,
Is there anything new?
Two more managers make their debut.

Back on Earth in the Bear's Lair, Octavius decided we were long overdue for a business review. The Caleb caper had thrown the normal flow of UUI activity off and he wasn't sure how well the overall company was faring. Time for a checkup and yet another Zoom conference. Organizer Maury was once more called into service. One of my less exciting duties. I started making contacts and set a session up for the following morning.

*****

Zoom time! A UUI get together. Universal Ursine Industries is a privately held enterprise, wholly owned by Doctor Octavius Bear, gazillionaire, Chairbear and CEO and his wife, The Bearoness Belinda Béarnaise Bruin Bear (nee Black). It is a true conglomerate in every sense of the word. Divisions, subsidiaries and affiliates all report in to the parent organization housed across the river in Kentucky.

On the screen this morning were the UUI corporate brass – Griselda Gorilla, President and COO; Roger Rottweiler, CFO; and Marty Marten, CIO. Also on hand was Wolford Wolverine, Octavius' Personal Lawyer and Chief Legal Officer of the Corporation. Bearoness Belinda, as co-owner was there and of course, little old me as Octavius' deputy.

Octavius wanted some separate time with the officers before bringing in the management of the divisions and subs.

"Good morning, all! In time honored tradition, I'll say it. "I suppose you're wondering why I summoned you all here." *(Gentle laughter)* Don't worry, no heads are rolling, no income reductions, no promotions or demotions, no new acquisitions, at least as far as I know. I hope no new lawsuits. *(The Wolverine shook his head. More gentle laughter.)* There is one rather nasty situation that I want to make you aware of but it can wait a bit until all the players have joined us."

"I just felt that after the Caleb Cassowary fiasco that almost put us in the dumpster, we should briefly meet and take stock, so to speak. You all know each other. I want to hear from you and then we'll invite the division, subsidiary and affiliate heads to join us. Griselda, what's the current outlook?

The COO grunted and said, "Octavius, we more than survived that damn Cassowary's assault. I won't say we're in better shape than if he hadn't pulled off his takeover attempt but business is looking up. Oddly enough, we got some good publicity out of our recovery efforts, A stable corporation able to withstand a nasty shock."

The Gorilla smiled, "Your assignment of Senhor Condor to the Advanced Super Computing Center was a masterstroke. He will give us the particulars but they are back in business with a vengeance. Our customers trust him."

"The other units are doing well. Consulting is a little behind but they are seasonal. Energy is looking up and I'm sure your personal friend, Chita will have good news about Media. We have no immediate acquisition news but we do have negotiations going on to bring on an airline. Wolford can give you the details. Our compensation program and HR policies are all on target. You can get a good night's sleep."

I looked over at Belinda. Sleep! Now would be the worst possible time for Octavius to have a narcoleptic episode. She winced but the Great Bear showed no signs of heading off to beddy bye. Whoosh!

He turned his attention to the CFO. "What's the money situation, Roger?"

"We've put aside reserves to cover the lawsuits but we're more than solvent. Our investments are paying off well and our tax situation is good. We won't have to go to the markets for loans except where the rates look profitable. Since we have no stockholders except our officers, we don't have any serious liabilities in that department."

Octavius smiled. *(I think it was a smile.)* "OK, Wolford, Let's hear it from Legal."

"As you know, courtesy of Caleb, we are being sued for damages by a wide variety of litigants. We're trying to get the suits consolidated. This will drag on for quite a while. I'm glad Roger has set aside reserves. I hope they are enough. The regulators are also on our case, both here and overseas. We've hired outside consultants to work with us. We'll be busy for quite a while."

The Bear snorted, "I guess it could be worse. Damn that bird. Marty, our faithful CIO, anything to report?"

"We are completely back in service, Doctor Bear. Thanks to Ursula, our files and backups are all clean of ransomware and our network transactions are back to normal. That covers all of our business systems here at UUI. You'll get separate reports from the Advanced Center and several of the subsidiaries. But generally, our processing abilities have been recovered."

"Well, that's good news. OK Maury, let's bring the rest of the team on board."

I poked at the touch screen and a stream of faces appeared. The Corporate officers stayed on. Thank goodness for large monitors. I called the roll in no particular order.

"Pharm and Pharma, UUI Logistics, UUI Consulting, UUI Medical and Genetics, UUI Energy, UUI Media, UUI Aerospace and the Advanced Super Computing Center. All aboard!"

Hello's, picture adjustments, sound tests and we were off and running.

Ormand Oryx, former Marketing Director of Pharm and Pharma had taken over the Division Directorship after the death of Dr. Llewelyn

Llama and the arrest of the Assistant Director for his murder. *(See Book Eleven – The Wurst Case Scenario)* He is spearheading the highly successful launch of the Division's "cultured meat" – Best Burgers and Best Wurst.

"Cultured meat is on a roll, Octavius. No pun intended. Consumers are literally eating our products up. The combined efforts of our chefs and your Frau Schuylkill and the advertising and publicity programs we launched with Chita have made us the market leader. Now we have to maintain that lead with more offerings, attractive packaging and special pricing for the big food chains. We're boosting our manufacturing and lab facilities."

"Our building materials, fabrics, medications and other food businesses are also thriving."

Octavius grinned to himself. Ormand's marketing background spurred his enthusiasms but he seemed to be a hard headed leader when it came to business decisions. "Thanks Ormand. Good Work."

"Who's next Maury?"

"Logistics"

This was the newest addition to the UUI family, an acquisition we made last year. Formerly known as White Horse Logistics after its founder and president, it is slowly but steadily assimilating into the UUI structure and culture. Sylvan Silver, named after the famous film star, neighed and flicked his mane on camera. "Delighted to be part of UUI, Doctor Bear. As you know, when it comes to logistics, trucking, air freight and shipping, we're number three. I won't be satisfied until we're number one and even then I won't be satisfied. Last year was a good year but this year looks even better. I hope we pick up the airline. We need more freighters. On-line purchases are driving our growth. We're supporting all the UUI divisions and subsidiaries, as well. Just watch us."

"Good one, Sylvan." Right now, Octavius was up to his foreshortened ears with a black horse, General Turmoil, but made no comments.

UUI Consulting was off to a slow start but that was typical. They relied on long and extensive engagements and government work. One large commitment had come to a satisfactory end but an end, nonetheless. New business took a lot of time to generate. The Great Bear knew about that world and had a lot of sympathy.

Next up was our old friend, Doctor "Odd" Vark UUI Chief Geneticist and Medical Director. "Greetings! As you know, I lead the Medical Support group at UUI Headquarters but I'm also in charge of the Genetics Lab at Polar Paradise sponsored jointly by the Bearoness and Ms. Catt. We're making significant strides in diagnosis and treatment of genetic disorders, infectious diseases and non-communicable diseases. I know you've been doing some genetic tinkering yourself, Octavius and of course, there is our little friend Otto with his unique talents bestowed on him by Imperius Drake. Where is Otto? Tell him I said, 'Hello.'"

The Great Bear didn't want to discuss either one of those subjects so we moved on to Energy. Actually, Energy specializes in land and water based wind turbines. They developed, manufactured, installed and maintain the equipment that supports the Hexagon. They also have major installations in Europe and both US coasts. Their Director is a Goose, the only other bird and a female at that, currently in a UUI executive position besides L. Condor.

HR was pushing for more species and gender diversity in the managerial ranks but Octavius had some deep seated distrusts of Avians, going back to Imperius Drake; the deadly but now dead Caleb Cassowary and of course, the denizens of Biosphere X. Gillian Goose, the Director of Energy, honked a greeting and launched into a pile of performance statistics. New installs were slow but maintenance was sustaining the revenue stream. The future, however. was definitely green.

Another female took up the screen, our own Ms. Catt-Chita-who in addition to being an Octavian also owned part of the Genetics Lab and managed the Media unit. Magazines, social media outlets, TV, film, news channels, games and entertainment, including the Cubs' Bold Brave Brilliant Bumptious Bears internet sensation. Oddly, no newspapers. Chita disliked the tabloid press. She winked at Octavius. "Hi, we're hauling in shekels by the bushel basket. Interactive everything! I'm sure we're making great contributions to your pension plan, Octavius, whenever you and the Bearoness choose to activate it." *(As usual, Chita was touching on a sensitive subject- this time, the Great Bear's retirement. Belinda may have put her up to it.)*

Octavius coughed. "Nothing I haven't come to expect from you. Ms. Catt. Bowls of champagne and tons of money. Keep a close eye on the Cubs, will you? That game of theirs may get out of hand."

"It won't on my watch, chief. They have immense talent. Scary actually! But we all have to keep them under control. Mlle Woof, the Bearoness, the Frau, Huntley, Maury, me and YOU! By the way, our issues of Purr and Sow with the Lion and Unicorn sold out in the first afternoon. We have a podcast planned for them. I think Preston Pavel Polar wants to create a film around them. They are absolutely unique and hot!"

"OK," said the Bear. "Things are looking good. I want to have a separate session with Aerospace and the Advanced Center. Thank you all. Before we sign off, I have some news to pass on to all of you. Those of you who were part of the UUI family a few years ago may remember the problems we had with an exoplanet called Biosphere X or the Home World. They almost destroyed us and UUI. Fortunately we headed them off."

"General Turmoil proceeded to destroy their governing body, their military and a good chunk of their infrastructure. Caleb Cassowary, that consummate trouble maker, after being caught in his extortion maneuvers against us, escaped from Earth and went to Home World to stir up those paranoids. He succeeded. Caleb is dead. I won't go into that now but he sowed seeds of vengeance and destruction on the exoplanet. They're plotting against Earth but once again, we're going to deal them a harsh blow. UUI is involved. I wanted all of you to know. We'll keep you posted. Thanks again! Aerospace and the Hex, please stay on."

Most of the screen inserts disappeared. Belinda and I stayed in the room with Octavius. Still on Zoom was Condo and his new assistant Li-Ping and the Director of UUI Aerospace, Leo Leopard. He joked that his name stood for **L**ow **E**arth **O**rbit.

Octavius frowned, "Gentlebeasts, I've been I touch with you separately so we can skip the reports. But we have a situation on our paws and claws. Caleb's attempt to destroy Earth's GPS was a near thing. I've had a few discussions with the Commanding General of Space Force and with General Turmoil of the Business. We all agree that the system is too damn vulnerable both in space and here on the ground."

"I've committed to putting significant resources-personnel, equipment and cash-into a major program to strengthen and protect our satellites and terrestrial stations with special emphasis on GPS. General Turmoil is matching our contribution and the Pentagon is working on an additional allocation over and above their current investments. Leo, I want you to head up our part of the program with significant help from the Advanced Super Computing Center, Condo."

"I'm sure those birds on Biosphere X have designs on the system. I hope we can head them off. You're aware of Project

Boomerang. It should knock them for a loop. We're ready to help a new regime recover, if there is one and it's not just a new set of fanatics. Otto is there monitoring and planning. Howard is getting ready to join him. We need to keep a close watch on events. That exoplanet is a disaster.

Chapter Thirteen

Preparations for war carry on.
Approvals are due whereupon
They will launch their assault.
There's one frustrating fault.
Just where has the Chancellor gone?

(The Home World)

Once more the Falcon Peregrine was shown into the Presence.

The Protector looked down from his opulent perch and screeched, "Report!"

"Progress, Your Worship. Excellent progress! We have acquired a suite of hardware and software designed to stage cyber attacks on our enemies and we are training a cadre of young avians in cyber warfare techniques."

"Where did this equipment come from? Who is doing the training."

"A Great Horned Owl from Gaea by the name of Mattingly. I mentioned him to you in our previous session. The Chancellor referred him."

"You have been in contact with the Chancellor?"

"Not directly, Sire. The Owl has shown us credentials and letters signed by the Chancellor and assures us that he will be returning in short order. He is negotiating with a secret organization on Gaea that supports all forms of cyber terrorism."

As usual, the Protector's paranoia was dominant. "Great Horned Owls are dangerous birds as are Cassowarys but I suppose ruthlessness is desirable under the circumstances. I will meet this Owl. Set up a Supreme Council meeting. Bring the military. Tell the Chancellor to return to the Home World forthwith. I shall want a demonstration of our capabilities."

"It shall be done, Sire. You will not be disappointed."

"See that I am not."

"I shall."

He bowed and hopped from the throne room. If Falcons could smile, he would. This will be the process that ensures Peregrine would become at least a Council Leader. Perhaps he would become the Chancellor. This Cassowary was not trustworthy. His personal ambitions ranged well beyond the Home World. First, the attacks must succeed and then he would see to Caleb's demise. Lord Peregrine! Protector Peregrine! It had a nice sound.

Chapter Fourteen

Our friend Mattingly comes to the fore,
He's a highly skilled bird but much more.
He's the General's spy.
A most slippery guy
Who is planning a fake Cyberwar.

(Back at the Bear's Lair)

"Octavius, we're connecting with Ursula 12 on Biosphere X. She's reporting in with interesting news."

"Thanks Howard. Maury, punch this up with the Octavians and Bruce Wallaroo."

"Hello Ursula. Hold on while we connect you to the team. How's it going? Is Otto OK?"

"He's fine. An unexpected development, Doctor Bear. It seems we have an ally here on the Home World."

The group formed up electronically and I gave Ursula the go ahead.

"Hello, everyone. Otto is tied up for the moment. I don't mean that literally. He's OK. We are hidden away in a forest near the capital. It seems the General has beaten us to the punch. He has a confederate here who is actively sabotaging the avians' plans for cyber warfare. Are any of you familiar with a Great Horned Owl called Mattingly?"

Over at the Hexagon, Condo stifled a laugh. "So that's where he is. Yes, Ursula, I know Mattingly. He's a high-tech mercenary. He's working for the General? I guess I'm not surprised. Like all of his species, he's a fierce and highly skilled raptor. In addition, he's a technological whiz. If he's taking on the Biosphere birds, they don't stand a chance."

She replied "He has them convinced that he is working for Caleb. They believe their Chancellor is alive, well and procuring attack mechanisms from a non-existent organization on Gaea that specializes in cyber warfare. He knows the Cassowary is dead but the birds are none the wiser. He doesn't know I exist and Otto and I want to keep it that way so I'm running in passive mode.'

"Otto and the Owl are hatching plans. A successful demonstration lulling the birds into a sense of unwarranted confidence followed by a backfiring disaster when they go live. Project Boomerang. I think Mattingly has an audience with the Protector and Supreme Council tomorrow. Otto plans to 'zap' in and remain hidden while the event takes place. The Falcon, Peregrine, who is spearheading the program has promised a display. The materials they think are coming from Caleb on Gaea are actually being supplied by the Business on Earth. The demo will go well. After they have signed off and poured more resources into it, the penny will drop. A runaway, self-inflicted cyber catastrophe. We'll be long gone when it happens."

Condo interrupted, "Tell Otto to watch his step. I don't entirely trust Mattingly although I doubt he would deliberately cross the General. He does too much business with The Business."

"For all his goofy looks and silly smiles, Otto is a very sharp and suspicious little guy. He's wary."

"Tell Otto to call in when he's free. I assume you two are not locked in with this Owl."

"Pretty close, Doctor Bear, but he has to keep up appearances with his avian clients."

Octavius snorted, "I guess I'll have to get back on the horn with the General. So much for letting me in on his plans. Thanks, Ursula. Keep hidden and tell Otto to stay safe. Give us a report on the audience and demo when they happen."

"Of course, Doctor Bear. Say hello to Byzantia for me."

Byzz had been listening in with Condo. She laughed. "Oh, Caleb would have a fit if he were still alive. Another disaster in the making. Good! Well. Back to Ursula 13. She's coming along quite well. A daunting lady!"

Belinda and the Octavians mused about the upcoming events. The Bearoness couldn't shake her concerns. She still remembered the Birds' near miss at fire bombing the Lair and UUI. Let's hope this Owl was as good as Condo seemed to think he was. But would anything short of total destruction rein those vengeful avians in? She thought not.

She went looking for the Cubs who were oblivious to all the intense activity going on around them. The game fully occupied their attention and they were applying their formidable intelligence to bringing off the new version. Gamers were a fickle and demanding bunch but all their new avatars, strategies and tactics should keep them happy for a while. Aunt Chita was handling the advertising and distribution. The Bold Brave Brilliant Bumptious Bears in Space! Little did they know how close they were to reality.

"Hi Momma! We're doing a beta test with our new characters. Jaguar Jack is a riot. The Frau is kinda stiff but we'll fix that. The real star is Uncle Preston Polar. He really belongs in space. His avatar is a really dangerous guy. You should get Poppa to use him on those nasty Home World birds."

"Aha," thought the Bearoness, "They are aware of what's going on. Next thing we'll know, they will want to travel with Otto and Howard to alternate universes. Octavius and I need to talk."

She replied to Arabella. "I don't think Uncle Preston would want to go space wandering. He's too busy making his blockbuster pictures. I think he's going to film Lion and Unicorn."

"Lion and Unicorn! They're in our game, too. Unicorn is fantastic! Wait and see."

Belinda pawsed, "At least, they don't want General Turmoil. They did say they wanted more villains. A complex character is Old Crazy Horse."

Chapter Fifteen

They're quite a formidable pair.
The General and the Great Bear!
It's a pretty safe bet
They won't stand for a threat.
The Home World had better beware.

Maury here. One more trip to the well. Setting up another Zoom session with General Turmoil. Telephone tag. Cloak and dagger identification procedures. Flunkies and bureaucrats. Finally! A black equine face on the screen.

"Turmoil here!" *(There usually is.)*

"Good morning, General. Maury Meerkat for Octavius Bear. I'll connect you."

Shifting screens, boops and beeps and the two Multiverse rivals faced off with each other. Octavius began the conversation.

"Well, General, it seems we have a joint effort going even though we never agreed on it."

"Ah, I see your operative has met Mattingly."

"Yes, he has. We know he is planning to disrupt the Home World plans for cyber warfare with flawed hardware and software supplied by you. He's pretending he's working with Caleb. The birds don't know he's dead. The Owl has a session scheduled with the Biosphere Supreme Council to explain and demonstrate how they can introduce malware and infections into Earth's systems. Otto is keeping in the background. I understand that Great Horned Owl is a technical genius."

"Yes, he is. He's also a deadly raptor. Some of those birds may not survive. Not that it bothers me very much. They're a vicious bunch. I thought I would keep quiet on this end and let things unfold for themselves. I see that has happened."

"A head's up would have been appreciated. After all, we informed you of Caleb's destruction."

"Well, if an apology is required, you have it. Now, let's do a little strategizing. Mattingly is setting up a series of malware attacks that will boomerang. Home World's technical infrastructure will go up in a cloud of smoke. The military will become non-existent; their power grids and communications capabilities will self-destruct. Finances will crumble. Supply chains will come crashing down. In short, what they plan for Earth will happen to them."

"The Protector and Supreme Council will probably be unseated or even killed off by rioting citizens. Mattingly plans to do away with that Falcon Peregrine who is managing the program in Caleb's absence. He's a nasty, ambitious twerp who has visions of grandeur for himself. No way. Now, is your minion - Otto, is that his name - prepared to assist?"

"Right now, they are plotting together. *(Octavius avoided any mention of Ursula who was Otto's ace in the hole if Mattingly turned out to be double dealing.)* Not sure how Otto feels about killing off Peregrine Otters are not raptors. He is sharp and aggressive but he's not bloodthirsty. On the other hand, those paranoid avians don't seem to be bothered by bringing on death and destruction. As you say, we may just want to sit back and let this little drama play itself out."

"I've used the Owl in the past. He is quite competent and trustworthy for a mercenary."

Octavius thought about that for a minute. Colonel Where had been a mercenary and Octavius trusted him with his and all the Octavian's lives.

"I assume you are getting reports from him on at least a daily basis."

"Oh yes, as well as requests for deadly material which we're shipping trans-space as we speak. We have quite a technological arsenal and Matt knows how to use it. He's even designed a few things himself.

Our confidence level is quite high on him although I always maintain backups and work-arounds. Our systems and personnel are all under careful scrutiny."

Once again, the thought occurred to me as it no doubt did to the Great Bear that working for the Business could get quite ugly. I'm glad our interactions were few and far between. I wonder how Byzz would have liked working for the General if she had accepted his offer. He probably saw her as a technically superior, cold-blooded killer. I hope he was wrong.

Octavius signed off and cut the connection.

He turned to me and said, "Let's get the Octavians together again. Bring Bruce, too. If Mattingly's destructive program is as complete as the General thinks it will be, we need a plan to deal with an exoplanet that is burning with even more vengeance than ever. They may not be able to wreak widespread havoc but they will still be able to mount individual assassination attempts. And you know who the targets will be."

I nodded and set myself up on the communications platform. Another live and Zoom session. Not quite herding cats but getting the team together took time. Finally, everyone was on board. The Cubs wanted to join in but Mlle Woof deflected them to the kitchens where snacks were sitting out, as usual. Huntley was getting quite proficient at creating bear cub temptations while the Frau was tied up in heading off nefarious schemes. He also was helping them with their Internet games. The Husky was becoming a Furball Favorite.

Octavius took command. "Folks, I thought I would bring everybody up to speed on what is happening on Biosphere X. As most of you know, Otto and Ursula are there, scouting out what those blasted birds are up to. It seems the late Caleb Cassowary left them with an instruction book on how to conduct a cyber war against Earth. A member of the Supreme Council, a Falcon named Peregrine, has taken on the assignment of making that happen. The Council and Protector believe

Caleb is still alive and negotiating on their behalf for malware and equipment on Gaea."

"Here's what's new. General Turmoil has stepped back into the picture and has commissioned a Great Horned Owl named Mattingly to act as Caleb's surrogate on the exoplanet. He is working with Peregrine to prepare for the great technological assault. He's actually a paid mercenary in the employ of the Business with major technology chops. He's setting up a system which will backfire on the birds and take out all of their major systems and apps. Probably trigger riots and coups. Condo is familiar with him."

The condor nodded and said, "He's a formidable character. He's worked for the General in the past with some startling results. Unless something unexpected happens, he will do major damage to Home World's infrastructure and more."

Octavius came back on. "Now, as we know all too well, the Biosphere bunch, after recouping and regrouping will not take this lying down. Large scale reprisals will be beyond their ability for quite a while but individual attempts at assassination will not. That's what I want you all to concentrate on. We need to build a defense strategy and individual protection plans."

Belinda interrupted. "Perhaps we should just get the General and this Owl to call off their sabotage. Couldn't Home World attack plans just fail?"

The Colonel snarled, "We believe the birds are too invested in their warfare scheme to back off. They'll keep trying if they just have a failure. They have to be shut down. That requires a disaster. Unless they are severely damaged, they'll continue to keep the war going. We learned that the last time. I'm not crazy about the General but this time I agree with him."

The Baroness flashed back, "Are you sure that's not just your military background surfacing, Wyatt? I, for one, am afraid. For the Cubs. For all of us. For Earth!"

Chita, who was not above a little killing when necessary. *(See Book Five – The Curse of the Mummy's Case)* chirped. "We will need to do a little assassinating ourselves, if the uprising's don't pan out. Get Otto to probe and see if there's a resistance group on Home World who are opposed to the Protector and Council's plans of conquest. I doubt if the whole planet is in love with mayhem. Some of them may be rational."

"He's on it already, Chita. The resistance is probably not well organized but that's where we can help. We'll need to convince them that the powers-that-be brought this on themselves and we're not the bad guys. That'll take some real convincing. But first things first. Mattingly is going to have to bring this off. What's your confidence level, Condo?"

"When it comes to cyber warfare, I'm glad he's on our side. I hope he doesn't turn. I wouldn't want to defend against him unnecessarily. Of course, we could but it would cost. We're still picking up after Caleb."

"There's a nasty thought. The General is not the most trustworthy of bosses. Let's hope he and the Owl have a good working relationship. Speaking of relationships, how are Otto and Mattingly getting along, Ursula?"

"Fine, Doctor Bear. You know Otto, diplomat extraordinaire. That silly smile covers for a very devious mind. I'm kind of devious, too.

"Don't we all know!"

Chapter Sixteen

Owl deceives with a trustworthy flair.
Pledging vengeance against the Great Bear
And the Horse, even more.
"I will settle the score
For all your disasters, I swear!"

Mattingly met with Councilor Peregrine to review the preparations to launch the first stages of the exoplanet's Cyberwar. He was careful to convince him that Caleb was energetically gathering resources on Gaea when in fact, carefully modified hardware and software (malware) was being imported to Home World from the warehouses and labs of The Business on Earth.

The Falcon fell for it. After all, wasn't the Owl a highly aggressive raptor endowed with sophisticated technical skills. Mattingly was going to be the enabler of Peregrine's aspirations. After their devastating assault on Earth, he'd skyrocket to first place among the Council members, those bureaucratic fumblers, and ultimately move to displace the Protector. He'd have to deal with Chancellor Cassowary who, no doubt, had similar intentions. Maybe he could bribe Mattingly to kill off Caleb. *(Little did he know that Caleb's remains were floating in space.)* Blinded by his fierce ambitions, the Falcon didn't realize how dreadfully outclassed he was by the Great Horned Owl in knowledge, experience and guile.

Hidden behind a curtain in the Falcon's chamber where he had 'zapped,' Otto along with Ursula 12, took in the conversation. The AGI was recording and transmitting the discussion back to Howard, Condo and Octavius.

"The first shipments have arrived from Gaea, Lord Peregrine. I have set the equipment up in our nondescript warehouse. I have been training several of your most trusted minions in the fine arts of hacking, cryptography, ransom, denial of service and malware. The computing part of the assault is forming up nicely."

"We still need to establish the telecommunications side of the program. Caleb plans to briefly hijack Gaea's satellites to blast targets on Earth, especially the Business and UUI. *(No such plan existed. Nor did Caleb.)* They'll never know what hit them and when they do realize what happened, they'll blame Gaea. That should stir up some serious trouble. Home World will have its revenge with no repercussions." The Owl hooted.

The Falcon was dazzled. His career was already well on its way but this would be the supreme event. The Owl was correct in calling him Lord Peregrine. No more the junior councilor, looked down on by those supercilious oafs. The Council and Protector would be figments of the past. Lord Peregrine would rule alone.

The military would be gutted and redesigned without that pompous Generalissimo and his aides. Technology would dominate. Chancellor Caleb would be gone but perhaps he would keep Mattingly Owl at his side.

But first, the demonstration must go on and then the attack must be launched and overwhelmingly succeed. History would record The Great Peregrine Interplanetary Cyber War – brief but devastating. Shock and Awe! Earth on its knees. The Bear and Odious Horse disposed of. The future looked magnificent.

Otto and Ursula could pick up none of the Falcon's internal fantasies but it was clear he had more on his mind than vengeance against Earth. He wanted absolute rule. Another Caleb. Nowhere near as brilliant and not that ambitious. He seemed content with ruling Home

World. Caleb wanted the Cosmos. But who knew? Ambition could be a malignant virus and Peregrine clearly had succumbed.

The Falcon cut off the discussion. He was in a hurry to report to the Protector. He needed his continued approval at least for the moment. Soon, he would need no one's approval.

The Supreme Council was in session. Otto 'zapped' into an ornate cupboard probably used for recording the daily proceedings. One of the Councilors was droning on about the rise in rebellious youth among the exoplanet's schools. Ursula quietly chimed. They needed to seek out a resistance movement on the planet. Was this a lead? Who was stirring up the young avians? The name Ezra kept coming up. Who is Ezra?

The discussion got no further because Peregrine Falcon flew into the chamber. The Protector cut off the speaker and turned to the junior councilor. "What do you have to report, Peregrine?"

"Great progress, sire. Chancellor Caleb has sent us a suite of hardware and software from Gaea to launch our Cyber-attack on Earth. Even as we speak, our volunteers are being trained in the arts of Cyber Terrorism by Mattingly Owl with great success. Our tests are working well."

"What is even more agreeable is the fact that the attack will take place using Gaea's telecommunication facilities. Earth will never know they have been assaulted by Home World but of course, we will know."

"One of the Councilors chirped and asked, "How will we know how much damage we have caused? Will we be avenged on that odious horse and arrogant bear?"

The Falcon laughed *(or what was the avian equivalent of laughter)* "We have arranged to position a damage assessment team on

Earth to survey the results. They will estimate the short term and long term destruction we have imposed. They will take special cognizance of General Turmoil and Octavius Bear along with their organizations. Our historians will have much to record. Much glorious revenge. Now, if you wish, you may accompany me to our war room and observe the program under development."

*****

Ursula was again relaying all this back to Earth. Octavius and the General were linked in on Zoom. On these calls, she pretended she was Otto. They didn't want the General or anyone else to know about the Ursula program if they could help it The Horse neighed. "Mattingly has identified those assessment team members. We'll scoop them up when the time comes. They're not here yet. Of course, they won't be reporting the results the Protector and the Falcon expect."

Octavius looked at the Zoom screen and asked, "Just how much do you trust that Owl? We're relying on him a great deal."

"Mattingly is one of my primary operatives. He's as skilled, experienced and trustworthy as they come. He's also as devious as that Otter of yours."

Otto and Ursula had already decided to search out Ezra as soon as Peregrine stopped his bragging. Otto needed to talk with the Owl. Who was Ezra and would he be of any use?

Peregrine had drawn a close to his self-congratulations, preened and marched over to his council seat. The Protector was clearly pleased. The other Councilors were not. Peregrine was a young, irresponsible hot head who was going to cause Home World a lot of trouble. Unfortunately, the Protector was buying into his braggadocio. He'd soon learn.

The Protector and Council rose and flew as a flock to the warehouse where Mattingly was working with his assault troops.

Otto 'zapped' out of the Council room undetected. "Let's track this Ezra down, shall we. But first, where might Mattingly be at the moment?"

The AGI responded. "Let's try that warehouse where they are setting up the attack scenarios. He's probably with his so-called trainee hackers and waiting for the Council and Protector to put in their beaks."

Ursula was right on. They arrived just as the birds from the Praesidium entered the large warehouse space for their demonstration. Peregrine was beside himself with ill-concealed glee. The soldiers rose from their terminals and bowed to the despot and his minions. The Protector waved them back to their seats and turned to the Owl. "I see you are well equipped. What are you going to show us?"

Neither he nor the Council would know a computer from a coffee machine. Of course, this didn't prevent the Protector from faking technical knowledge. The Owl greeted them and played along with the pretense. Hidden in a corner, Otto and Ursula listened in.

"Felicitations, Your Highness! Greetings, Gentlebirds. Welcome to Cyberwar Central. We are ahead of schedule in our preparations. We are still awaiting a few small pieces of communication hardware but all else is installed and we are working with the malware that will be used in the attack."

"We will be using the networks of Gaea to stage our assault, thus cloaking Home World's identity. Once the communication hardware is complete we will engage in a series of tests. Right now, we are simulating the network hookups."

"Councilor Peregrine has selected the finest birds on this biosphere to staff this project. You should be very proud of them. True Cyberwarriors all!" *(The Owl was laying it on pretty thick.)* Peregrine puffed up at the compliment.

The Protector looked at the Council members and then addressed Mattingly. "I, of course, am highly familiar with the latest developments in malware. What programs are you using?"

The Owl grinned to himself. "I'll let one of your splendid combatants answer that, Lord Protector." He pointed at a kestrel who was intensely stabbing away at his touchscreen. The bird looked up, gulped and in a quavering chirp, addressed the great lord."

"This is special dark denial of service software designed, developed and coded by Chancellor Caleb himself. It is vastly superior to anything available on the clandestine market. Its cryptography is literally unbreakable and its speed of execution is breathtaking. It will be our primary weapon of attack, crashing Earth's systems and tying up files and applications throughout the entire Internet. It is quite deadly."

All this was true with two exceptions. The technicians of The Business designed and implemented the software and the target was Biosphere X, not Earth. Only three individuals in the room knew that. Mattingly, the cleverly hidden Otto as well as Ursula 12.

The Protector bored easily and the Council showed signs of wanting to return to the Praesidium. Sensing this, Peregrine made a short speech summarizing the plan and timetable and promising the great disaster that would befall earth and then later Gaea. The Protector smiled his buzzard smile, motioned to the Council and flew from the room.

The Otter emerged from his hiding place. Mattingly Owl was moving from workstation to workstation, directing, correcting and detecting. The hackers were assiduously setting up their attack scenarios, simulating and testing. They didn't notice the shadowy presence in the corner of the room but the sharp-eyed Owl did. He moved away from the action and hopped over into the dark corner, "Oh ho, who have we here?"

Ursula was in passive mode, once again recording the action as it took place. Otto came up with one of his grins. "Hi Mattingly! I'm back from Earth and Octavius Bear. He says hello by the way. The General knows who I am. It looks like you have Project Boomerang well in hand."

"What are you doing here?"

"Reconnoitering. After you get through making a mess of this planet, we'll probably have to pick up the pieces. We know the General has no intention of fixing things up or calling the program off."

"Not likely, my mammal friend. There's nothing you can do to stop it either, if that's what you have in mind."

"No, we want to see the Protector and the Council shot out of their perches. This guy Peregrine is a real loser. We just don't want to see rampant carnage and destruction."

"It's necessary if we want to shut these natural born aggressors down. Are you sure Caleb is no more?"

"All gone! The universe is a lot safer with him disposed of."

The Owl hooted gently, "Look, we have to ensure the Protector and Council don't survive. I don't like the idea of females and chicks being hurt but we have to get the populace sufficiently overwhelmed that they do something drastic."

Otto replied, "I'm on my way to meet with Ezra Eagle. He seems to be a likely candidate to head up a new government."

"I haven't met that bird but I know he gives the Council fits. I'm surprised he's still alive."

"I hope he is. See ya!" ZAP!

The Development of Civilization-Volume 14
Part 4
Hacking, Spoofing and Rootkits
(From "An Introduction to Faunapology" by Octavius Bear Ph.D.)

In the history of computing, "hacking" did not start out as the pejorative term we regard it as today. It simply referred to the efforts of technologists to overcome or work around issues in design and implementation of systems, applications and basic code. It was often a synonym for troubleshooting. Times have changed.

Today, we regard hacking as an aggressive activity designed to compromise digital devices, such as computers, smartphones, tablets, and even entire networks. Hackers are assumed to be motivated by antagonistic intentions whether for personal or institutional gain, hostility, or just to prove they are smarter than the average member of the computing or communicating community. They use a wide variety of tools but rely heavily on flaws in their target environments – weak passwords; unintentional backdoors; poorly selected software; uncontrolled access and hardware/firmware shortcomings in design and/or implementation.

"Spoofing" is the act of disguising a communication from an unknown and usually hostile source as being from a known, trusted source. Spoofing can apply to emails, phone calls, and websites, or can be more technical, such as computer to computer protocols or processes. How often has a malicious individual tried to get your passwords or personal IDs through fraudulent phone or e-mail scams and social engineering tactics like "phishing?"

Spoofing can be used to gain access to a target's personal information, spread malware through infected links or attachments, bypass network access controls, substitute passwords, or increase traffic to crash systems or create denial-of-service or larger cyber-attacks.

Such attacks on organizations can lead to infected computer systems and networks, data breaches, and/or loss of functions and revenue. In addition, spoofing that leads to the rerouting of internet traffic can overwhelm networks or lead clients to malicious sites aimed at stealing information or distributing malware.

What's a rootkit? Sounds like a vegetable but it's much nastier than rutabaga (or even broccoli).

A "rootkit" is a collection (kit) of malicious software, designed to enable unauthorized access to a computer, its access control software or accounts (roots.) It's a version of malware.

Rootkit installation can be automated, or an attacker can install it after having obtained root or Administrator control. It is then possible to hide the invasion and develop privileged access. With full control over a system, existing software can be modified, destroyed or replaced, including software that might otherwise be used to detect or circumvent the rootkit thus making discovery difficult or impossible.

Reinstallation of the operating system and/or browser may be the only available solution. In the case of firmware rootkits, it may be necessary to replace hardware.

In other words, rootkits are truly vicious.

UUI and the Advanced Computing Center are both engaged in developing and distributing defenses against all of these Cyber Attacks.

Chapter Seventeen

Will the Boomerang plot really work?
Is the Peregrine bird such a jerk?
Will his ambitious dream
Make him fall for the scheme?
Then will Biosphere X go berserk?

(The Bear's Lair)

Octavius called up Condo. "Senhor Condor, give me the benefit of your technical smarts. What's your opinion of this Boomerang stunt this Owl Mattingly is planning? Will it work?"

"It can, Doctor Bear. It all depends on how they've rigged the attack software and firmware. The Business technicians are very competent. The whole question is whether Mattingly can sneak the tainted code into the birds' systems without it being detected. They're not very technically savvy. If he can and I believe it's possible, then he needs a trigger to set the disaster off. Instead of using Gaea's telecom facilities, he needs to link their cyber terror software to the Home World's own network and clouds in such a way that they literally self-destruct. Right now, the warfare systems are probably isolated from everything else. The Owl has to get them connected. I suggest we have a skull session with Ursula. I'm sure she's been scanning the entire process."

"Good, contact Otto and have the two of them link in with us on Zoom."

"Hang on. I'll make the connections. Who else do you want on the call?"

"Howard, Marlin, the Colonel and the Frau. Maury and Bruce are here with me. Get Byzz in on this. I want to hear from her and see if she's playing straight."

"She's up to her ears in Ursula 13 development. Happy as can be but she's got a good sense for cyber war. I'll link her in. How long are you going to keep Otto out there?"

"I want to get him back soonest but there's this Ezra he's been talking about. A sort of rebel leader if I understand correctly. If this ploy by Mattingly works, we're going to need someone to pick up the pieces. Ezra won't be happy about the destruction but he may see it as a way to topple the Protector and Council. We'll have to play it carefully. I'm not sure this Mattingly or General Turmoil are much interested in restoring Biosphere X. I am. Not all those birds are bloodthirsty paranoids. We need to stabilize, not destroy. I may need you to lead a repair team."

Condo replied, "You may want to consider Howard, Maury or Otto for that. I'm close to being overwhelmed here at the Hex. Caleb left quite a mess.'

"Sorry. It's just that you're so damned competent that I keep going to you. I'm overdoing it. Well, let's gather the troops."

*****

It took a few minutes to get everyone online. Otto had 'zapped' to a neutral location away from the birds and Mattingly Owl. Ursula 12 was up on both ends of the link. I called the roll. Everyone was on deck.

Octavius opened the discussion. "First off, Otto and Ursula. Does Mattingly know what he's doing and can he be trusted?"

Ursula responded first, "He's more than competent, Doctor Bear. I've been analyzing his activities and it looks to me as though he's got this whole plan under perfect control. We have no reason to distrust him at the moment. The hackers that he's training are following his instructions but they are a wild card in all this. If they do what they're told, it will come off as he plans. If not, it's anybody's guess. It's a shame this has to happen."

"How many hackers are there?"

Otto replied, "Five plus the Owl. They've been recruited from the military but the Army officers have no part in the exercise In fact, the Generalissimo resisted giving them over. The Protector won out."

Ursula came back, "Speaking of the Protector, I think he's getting suspicious of the fact that Caleb hasn't returned. Supposedly, he's on Gaea masterminding all this. The Protector has issued orders for his return. I'm not sure how much longer Mattingly can keep him at bay. He needs to come up with a credible story."

"When does the attack begin?"

Otto replied, "The last phony telecom gear showed up. They'll be ready in in about 24 Earth hours. Ursula and I need to make contact with this Ezra before then. It turns out, he's an Eagle. We're not going to warn him. We don't know where his sympathies lie. We just want to hear what he has to say about rebellion and judge whether he could lead a planetary recovery. We think he's eager to throw over the Protector and the Council but I doubt he'll be very happy about the destruction the Boomerang cyber-attack will cause."

"If we send Howard to join you, can you hide him?"

"For 24 hours we certainly can."

"What do you think, Howard. Want to join Otto and Ursula?"

"And do what?"

"Help plan out a recovery program once the powers-that-be are no longer."

"I can but first let's scout out this Ezra. By the way, what is Mattingly going to do once the trigger is pulled?"

"As far as we can tell, he plans to get the hell out of there and return to Earth posthaste. At least that's what the General has instructed him to do. They have no interest in cleaning up the mess they're going to make."

"Seems to me, we are always mopping up after the General."

"I agree but we can't let those birds go on a galactic frenzy. Otto, Ursula! Find this Ezra and let's see which way the Home World wind is blowing. I assume he has associates. He may even have established a political party although I can't imagine the Protector would tolerate it. Let's see what he's capable of."

"If we're going to fix this mess, the leadership has to come from within the planet. It can't be us. We can help but we can't control the process. Give me an assessment. Is this Ezra the bird we want to back? If not, who else is there? I doubt if any Council member or an officer in the military would be a likely candidate but who knows."

"Don't tell Mattingly what you're doing. He'll get back to the General and we'll be at each other's throat. Good luck!"

Chapter Eighteen

Ezra Eagle's on household arrest
And our Otto's creating a test
Is he really sincere?
Is a new regime here?
As a leader, would he be the best?

It took Ursula about twenty seconds to locate Ezra's aerie on the outskirts of the Capital. It took Otto another twenty seconds to 'zap' to the entrance. There were two government guards at the portal. They hadn't noticed him…yet. With Ursula in passive mode recording the event on his laptop, he scanned the interior. The Eagle was on his perch but no one else was in sight. Time for another 'zap.'

Ezra looked up in surprise at the Otter's sudden appearance but kept his cool. No violent reaction although with those mean looking talons, he would be a formidable opponent. Otto was ready to 'zap' again but hung in there.

"Who are you and what are you doing in my home? You're not avian. Get out or I'll call the guards. How did you get in here? What do you want?"

Otto flashed one of his goofy grins and said, "Questions, questions! Stay calm please, Eagle Ezra, and all will be revealed. My name is Hairy Otter and since I am not a bird, it should be obvious that I'm not from your world. I mean you no harm. In fact, I may be able to do you some good. As to how I got here, just let's say I teleported from an alternate universe. Do you believe in alternate universes?"

"Of course! I am not a naïve chick. Are you from Earth, Gaea or elsewhere?"

"Let's not go into that for the moment. I am told that you are the leader of a faction that is dissatisfied with the current ruling class here on Home World."

"That is hardly news. I and my associates have been jailed several times for sedition. I am currently under house arrest. That's why I'm alone here. How did you get past the guards? Are they still outside my aerie?"

"Yes, they are. They seem bored out of their minds which is good. We can have a nice little chat and perhaps reach an agreement that will help you."

"Why should you help me? How do I know you're not a government spy?'

"To answer your second question first. I'm not, but you're going to have to trust me. I grant you that's not a particularly prudent thing for you to do but at the moment, it looks like you're not getting much assistance from your associates who seem to be in the same situation."

He continued. "Now, why should we help you? Because we have reason to believe the Council and Protector intend to launch a cyber-attack on several planets. We hoped to stop them, especially a Falcon named Peregrine and we could have used your knowledge and influence to make that happen. *(No mention of the Boomerang process being developed by Mattingly.)*

"Ah, yes, Councilor Peregrine. A hopped up egotist whose ambitions are running away with him. I think he has ambitions to be the next Protector."

"Do you share his ambitions?"

"Not I. I want to see the whole Council structure eliminated and replaced by elected representatives. Right now, the Council serves at the Protector's whim and its members are appointed by him for lifetime positions. Unless, of course, they anger him. He's a despot. We Eagles were once the nobility of Home World. Now we are reduced to menial jobs or no jobs at all."

"Do you just want to take over and repopulate the Council with Eagles?"

"No, my Otter friend. I want the avians of this planet to make their own choices for whomever governs them. Free elections. Repeal of the dictatorial edicts we live under. Replacements within the military and elimination of the Secret Police. Most of all, I want to see an end to the aggressive paranoia that besets this world. We are making ourselves miserable and creating cosmic enemies."

*****

Ursula was relaying this dialogue to the Octavians. Reactions varied from acceptance to serious doubt. Howard thought we might be able to work with Ezra and his associates. The Wolves were more dubious. "He could just be another tyrant in the making."

The Great Bear nodded. "We don't have many choices. The current regime is extremely dangerous and this Peregrine Falcon sounds like a budding dictator. We have to isolate and unseat them or continue to live our lives under severe threat. After destroying their resources ala the Turmoil/Mattingly plan, Biosphere X will be a hotbed of hostility. We need a stable and peaceable group in charge. Otherwise, revenge will be the order of the day."

"Isn't Mattingly's plan designed to put the blame on the Falcon, The Council and the Protector?"

"Yes, but that story needs to have airtight credibility. They'll wonder when the Owl disappears and Caleb never returns. Earth will be a prime suspect. Let's get Otto back here and strategize."

*****

Ursula's chime rang. Otto got the message. Time to return to Earth.

The Eagle peered around. "What was that sound?"

The Otter smiled, "Just my laptop resetting itself. Well, Ezra. *(I hope you don't mind my using your first name.)* I think I have enough information for the moment. I'll be back along with several of my colleagues. Let's see what we can do about lifting your house arrest. Meanwhile, stay safe. I'll just teleport past those guards out there."

"Wait, you never told me where you were from."

"And I'm not going to. Let's just leave it at 'another planet.' One of many who are not well pleased with your Home World rulers. See you soon."

ZAP!!

Chapter Nineteen

What to do about Biosphere X?
Can we unseat the Protector Rex?
If we help Ezra win
Will more troubles begin?
It's a problem that's very complex.

(Back at the Bear's Lair)

Down in the Multiverse Lab, Otto made another one of his not-so-soft landings. He shook his head, checked for Ursula on his laptop, looked around at Howard and Marlin and croaked "Ta-Da! Back from another hard day at the office!"

Octavius rumbled in along with the Colonel and Frau and said, "Welcome back, Otto, Ursula. Well done! You may have to do a quick turnaround if the General's plans come off. I just want to stop the cyberattack by the Home World fanatics. He wants to destroy the whole planetary infrastructure. If he and his Owl succeed, we will have a real mess to help clean up."

The Colonel snorted, "Why should we care? Biosphere X has been a thorn in our side for years. They are bringing this on themselves. They deserve what they get."

The Bear replied. "That's certainly true of the current government. I suppose paranoia and a deep sense of vengeance are planetary traits but a lot of innocent birds are going to be hurt courtesy of those idiots if the General has his way. This will just prolong the conflict. We need some way of shutting the violence down permanently. The Multiverse is messy enough as it is. I need to talk with the General again. Otto, Ursula, what's the story with this Ezra Eagle?"

The AGI responded, "We can't be sure but he's the best alternative we have at the moment. The Council is a washout. Peregrine is a major threat blinded by his own ambitions and the Protector is living on borrowed time. If we can't stop the Owl's activities, we'll have a massive repair program on our paws. "

Otto agreed. "I only spoke with Ezra for a brief few moments but his intentions are to recast the whole planetary structure around free elections and open government. I know, lots of would-be reformers have turned out to be worse than their predecessors but the current regime can't be allowed to continue. I'd say we should cautiously support him, assuming, of course that the populace does. He could end up being another tyrant. We're never going to be able to write off that exoplanet. It's a permanent world of trouble for Earth."

"What about Gaea?"

"Gaea seems to be on Home World's back burner. That may change when they realize Caleb isn't there and never will be."

"What about it, Byzz? Until recently, you were a pseudo-Gaean. Is the Gaea government stable? Will Biosphere X be able to undermine their peaceful existence? BTW, how goes the Ursula 13 project?"

The Bonobo replied. "If we can unseat the Home World hierarchy, the new administration will probably be too busy picking up the pieces in their own bailiwick to go after Gaea. Besides, didn't Otto say this Ezra is a peace loving bird?"

Otto chuckled. "I sure hope so. I also hope he takes over. We'll just have to ride with it. After we clean up the General's disaster. "

Byzz came back. "Doctor Bear, Condo. Ursula 13 is about ready for some trial runs. Suppose I put 12 and 13 together to repair the Home World technology?"

Octavius snorted. "We can use all the help you can give us. What do you think, Condo?"

"Sounds reasonable. What's your opinion, Ursula 12?"

"Bring her on. We'll make a great team."

Chapter Twenty

Project Boomerang's off like a shot.
The attackers don't really know what
Is at fault and just why
Cyber War's gone awry.
Was it something their test plan forgot?

Mattingly had set the attack group up for the big event and called on Peregrine Falcon to lead the assault. The Councilor hopped into the warehouse where the hacker recruits were going through their final boot up procedures.

"Is everything in readiness, Owl? There can be no mistakes. The Protector and Supreme Council have very high expectations. Where is Chancellor Caleb? He should be here to witness this. It was his proposal but I have brilliantly brought it to fruition."

"Of course, Lord Peregrine." *(What a pompous, egotistical jerk. Caleb and Peregrine. A matched pair. They would have killed each other off by now.)* "The Chancellor has been detained on Gaea but we must seize the moment. He will see the results."

"Yes, yes. Just a moment. I want to address the recruits."

"By all means, Councilor!"

"Attention, Birds of Home World, you have been chosen and trained for a mission of cosmic importance. Today, under my leadership, we will wreak vengeance on our enemies on Earth in such a way that they will never fully recover. Our cyberattack will be devastating and total in its impact. They will never know what hit them nor will they know from whence it came. But we will know and rejoice. The Protector and Supreme Council await the splendid news. Are you all ready with your assignments?"

A chorus of tweets, chirps and hoots!

"Then proceed!"

*****

Amid the clicking keyboards, skittering mice and avian outbursts, Peregrine failed to notice that Mattingly was no longer there. Indeed, he was well on his way back to Earth to report, collect his fees from General Turmoil and make himself scarce in case something didn't go according to plan. But he had no doubts. Project Boomerang had been carefully constructed by the technicians of the Business, populated with deadly self-destruct malware and installed meticulously by the Owl. He played on the bloodthirsty nature of the recruits and trained them only to the extent that they could launch the program but not trouble shoot or mitigate the self-inflicted pain that was about to result.

The General's technicians had built tracking algorithms into the malware to report the damage being inflicted. The Business would know exactly what happened. Home World would experience but not understand the results

On his way to Earth, Mattingly wondered what became of the Otter. He had probably returned to Octavius Bear to check in. The Owl would leave it up to the General to inform the Ursine Gazillionaire of the results. Mattingly would return to his opulent lodge in the North Woods and relax until his next assignment came along. Hopefully, not for a while. This one had been a beaut.

*****

"Councilor Peregrine, we have a problem."

The Falcon frowned at the two young hawks who fluttered their wings to get his attention. "Yes, what is it?"

"We can't establish communications. The links to Gaea we have set up to transmit our attack codes to Earth aren't responding. *(Way to go, Mattingly!)*

"I don't understand. Those connections were established and tested thoroughly by the Owl. Where is that Bubo Virginianus?

"He's not here, Councilor."

"You, Kestrel! Find him! The rest of you, reset the system! Immediately!"

"The Restart isn't working. Neither is the Shut Down function. Our keyboards, monitors and mice are locked."

"Pull the power circuit breakers."

The lights and peripheral units in the depot went dark but the system hummed on. "It's running independently. What's it doing? How is it doing it?"

What it was doing became immediately apparent outside the darkened warehouse. Within seconds, across the exoplanet, all communication ceased. New passwords were automatically inserted on major financial, manufacturing, supply chain, medical, governmental, military, education, transportation and infrastructure management applications. The Home World Cloud began formatting all files, including backups.

The planetary power grid overloaded, starting a series of blazes and explosions. Buildings caught fire. Accidents broke out on streets, highways and intersections. Spontaneous riots built up as thousands of birds flew to the Capital to investigate and demand government action.

Rage, confusion and fear combined to cast the Supreme Council into a catatonic state. The Protector tried to call in the military but there was no immediate response. Their communications systems were all down. Finally, the Generalissimo got a small cadre together and marched to the Praesidium where a number of the soldiers promptly joined the rioters.

Questions! Conspiracy Theories! Paranoia! A disaster! No accident! Deliberate! Who had attacked them? What was the Council going to do? Calls for mass resignations starting with the Protector. Protector, Ha! He couldn't safeguard a nest of fledglings, let alone a vulnerable exoplanet. They were surrounded by enemies and led by idiots. Time for change. Violent change! Strike down the Council! Kill the Protector!

*****

Back on Earth, Octavius put through yet another Zoom call to the General. "What's the verdict?"

"Project Boomerang is succeeding well beyond our expectations. Home World is in a state of chaos. Our technicians and the Owl did an outstanding job. Mattingly is back here on Earth and of course, you say Caleb's body is floating among the satellites and asteroids. A revolution is in process. The government is collapsing. The Protector will be lucky if they don't string him and the entire Council up. That ambitious fool Peregrine is not long for his world."

"Sounds like we have some cleaning up to do. Signing off."

*****

On the outskirts of the Capital city, an Eagle briefly sat in darkness, then got down from his perch to reconnoiter the situation. He was no more aware of all the damage and uproar on Home World than the rest of the populace. He flew down to the entrance of his aerie where he was under house arrest. His guards were nowhere to be found. He prepared to take wing and fly to the Praesidium but was suddenly confronted by two grinning faces – a Porcupine and that mercurial Otter. "Hi Ezra. I'm back. Meet my associate, Howard Watt. We just flew in from Earth. We didn't cause this catastrophe. We're here to help. We can probably put most of this cyber chaos back in order. Looks like your big chance has arrived. The planet needs a leader!"

"What happened?"

"Home World has been the victim of Project Boomerang, a cyberattack gone horribly wrong for your side. Chancellor Caleb persuaded your Protector and Council that birds were destined to dominate the cosmos and as I told you, set up a plan for waging cyberwar against Earth, then Gaea and then more and more exoplanets. An Owl named Mattingly was charged with developing the attacks under Councilor Peregrine's supervision. What he and the Council didn't know was that Mattingly works for General Turmoil. Remember him and the damage he wreaked on your planet in retaliation for a series of raids Home World staged on Earth?"

"As I mentioned the last time we met, we came here to stop the war but we were too late. Peregrine triggered the attack but what he and the Council didn't know was the General's technicians and the Owl created a process that laid waste to this planet instead of Earth. Project Boomerang!"

"Howard and I are here to undo the technological damage to the extent we're able. You and your associates will have to handle the social, political and physical destruction and recover however you can. Are you up for it?"

"I am and I will"

The Eagle nodded at the two of them and took flight. He stopped momentarily to call and assemble the leaders of his party – Home World Free – and told them to meet him at the Praesidium. They had been under house arrest but their guards had also disappeared at first sign of the disaster.

Their chance had come and he would not allow it to elude him.

Chapter Twenty One

The Protector's convinced it's a plot.
And he's furious - why ever not?
But to save his life span
He must scuttle the plan
Hatched by Peregrine, that rotten swot.

In the Council Chamber of the Praesidium, panic was the order of the day. Several members had already flown the coup that was violently progressing. Most of the guards had disappeared. The military had failed. The Council was no longer safe.

The Protector had rapidly concluded that the destruction taking place across the planetary landscape was somehow linked to Chancellor Caleb, Peregrine Falcon and that shifty Horned Owl. It was a plot. A cybernetic plot carried off by a small group of conspirators. In the guise of a cyberattack on Earth and Gaea, they had engineered the overthrow of the Home World government and were causing unbelievable damage in their wake.

He escaped into an inner chamber and summoned his aide, Goshawk. "This is Peregrine's doing. That ambitious fowl wants the Protector's perch and he doesn't care how he goes about getting it. Find him and bring him here. Bring his technical team as well. Get that Horned Owl. Don't be too gentle."

He didn't know where Caleb was. He had been mysteriously absent for quite some time. Maybe Peregrine had done him in. And what happened to that Owl? He was the technical genius. He was needed to stop the electronic carnage. Peregrine probably didn't know how.

Things were going from bad to worse.

*****

Down at the Praesidium Plaza, an avian horde had grown to uncontrollable proportions and threatened to set fire to the building. The few members of the police and army who had stayed on were in no way capable of dealing with the situation.

Suddenly, a dark, winged figure soared over the pulsating mob and landed atop a statue of one of the early Protectors. A few protesters saw him and then more. A shout went up. "Ez-Rah, Ez-Rah, Ez-Rah!" The Eagle shrieked loudly. "Stand down, my friends. Don't make the damage worse. I and my associates will deal with immediately restoring the planet's infrastructure. You know you can trust me. This is all the result of a cyberwar plot against Earth and Gaea by the Protector and the Council that went dreadfully wrong. They will be unseated, arrested and punished. I will form a new temporary government until free elections can be conducted. I will then resign and will not stand for election." *(Shouts of No, No, No! Take Control! Take Control!)*

"No, we have had enough of individual rule by despots and their cronies. Representative government is not easy to set up but we must try. I call on all of you to assist me. Meanwhile, go back to your aeries and nests and we will go about the business of restoring power, communications, infrastructure, business and medical facilities. What is left of the Army will be engaged in making repairs. We have a team of technically skilled friends who will be assisting us."

"Ez-Rah! Ez-Rah! Ez-Rah! Ez-Rah! Ez-Rah! Ez-Rah!"

Otto, Howard and the two Ursulas were watching this from a niche in the Plaza. The Porcupine said. "That sounds like us. Let's get over to that warehouse Peregrine set up and get those rogue systems under control. Are you ready, Ursula 12 ? How about you, 13?"

12 responded. "It's a tall order. That Owl and the techies from the Business created quite a mess. Let's get over there. First order of business – undo the malware. Then restore the networks. I thought after Caleb's caper at UUI that I'd had enough of cleaning up electronic

swamps. Now this. But if it changes the Home World for the better, it might yet be worth it. We need to deal with Ezra. Their Army and support groups are going to have to deal with the physical destruction. He needs to head that up."

Ursula 13 rang her chime and agreed. "I'll deal with the passwords. My quantum circuits are specially designed to solve cryptographic problems. You may want to take on the overloads and rebalance the traffic. Before we do anything, we'll have to get rid of those "cyberwarriors" if they're still there."

It turned out they had all run in a panic. They were rightfully afraid they would be killed if they were found on the spot.

*****

The Protector was still hidden in his inner chamber awaiting the return of his aide with the hapless Peregrine. The door slammed open and the Falcon was thrown on the floor in front of the despot. His aide and two members of the Secret Police stood over him. "We caught him, Lord Protector, preparing to leave the city. What do you wish done with him?"

"Well, you ambitious idiot. What have you to say? Did you deliberately engineer this disaster to cause my overthrow and the downfall of the Council?"

"No, My Lord, certainly not. I am a loyal member of the government and unconditionally dedicated to you as our ruler. *(Liar, Liar! Tail on Fire.)* We have been duped by that odious Chancellor and his toady, the Owl. I don't know where either of them is?"

The Protector turned to his aide. "Goshawk, where is Chancellor Cassowary?"

"He is not on Gaea, My Lord. We have scoured that planet and he is nowhere to be found. We believe that this Falcon did away with him to take over his position."

Peregrine shrieked, "What? No! I worked closely with the Chancellor."

"Where is the Owl?"

"We think he has left the planet, My Lord. He and the cyber attackers are all gone."

"Peregrine, answer this carefully. Your life depends on it. How do you propose to restore all this wreckage? Do you know how?"

The Falcon was silent.

The buzzard shrieked. "You are a traitor. You have plotted to bring me down. Now, you will feel my vengeance. Guards, kill him."

Three shots rang out. One instantly killed Peregrine. Two shattered the body of the Protector.

Goshawk screamed, "Death to insane tyrants. Killers of chicks and females." He turned to the two guards. "Let us go. Leave these bodies here for the mob. The Council is next."

Chapter Twenty Two

The Octavians come on the scene
And the damage is hardly routine.
They must use all their skill,
As they certainly will,
To control this fierce cy-war machine.

At the now empty and darkened warehouse, the Octavians found the servers and terminals still humming away, locked in their destructive onslaught. There were no signs of the hackers and Mattingly had long ago returned to Earth. They wondered what had happened to Peregrine. If they were going to start setting things back to rights, they did not want him interfering. He probably had made himself scarce. Little did they know that he and the Protector had breathed their last, their bullet-riddled bodies lying in a secret room in the Praesidium waiting to be discovered by a raging horde.

Ursula 13 looked at Otto. "OK, first thing, we have to regain control of these units. Mattingly has them operating on battery power and locked in the 'On' position. We need to shut them down and then boot them back up in a clean condition. Then I can start working on undoing the ransomware.

Ursula 12 started on the networks. Several of the terminals were generating immense traffic volumes of useless messages whose only purpose was to crash the public and private servers. She intercepted the software producing the overloads and cut off the flow.

Suddenly a winged shadow descended over the area. Peregrine? No, it was Ezra. "I thought I'd find you here. Can you bring this under control?"

Otto responded. "It's going to take some time. I have two diagnostic computers *(the unidentified Ursulas)* at work analyzing the situation. Howard and I have been able to stop the denial of service activities but we have to purge all those useless messages and transactions."

"Getting the systems, applications and files back is going to take some massive decryption of the malware that has captured them. Our technology is competent and fast but the damage is pretty extensive. What's happening on the physical front?"

"There are still small mobs trying to enter the Praesidium. I have been trying to calm them but some of them want to string up the Council and Protector. Can I tell them that you are making progress?"

Howard replied, "Oh yes. We believe we'll have the power grids back up in short order, the water plants and then the global communication systems. That should calm things a bit. Were there any casualties or fatalities?"

"Too many! Fires and accidents! Hospital deaths! I can't help sympathizing with the mob. Those arrogant fools on the Council thought they could destroy Earth and they ended up killing off Home Worlders by the score. They'll be brought to justice but not gang justice, if I can help it. I must return to the Praesidium. Thank you for your wonderful assistance. You will be declared Heroes of the Biosphere."

Not exactly what we had in mind.

He flew off and our team returned to its tasks of electronic sanitation and restoration.

Time to issue another report to Octavius.

*****

Maury here! The Great Bear and I were sitting with the Frau and Colonel when the call came through from Otto and Howard. Ursula 12 was doing the relaying. Ursula 13 was still engaged in cleaning out Mattingly's ransomware. Otto stared at us with his perennial grin. "Hello, Earth! Home World is still quite a mess but we're getting some of its technology back. Not sure about the physical damage. Ezra Eagle has said he'll take care of that."

"Thanks Otto! Howard, What's your take on the Eagle?"

"My jury is out. He sounds credible and he's taking the recovery program on with a lot of energy. He has a political party-Home World Free-made up primarily of eagles. Not sure how big or influential it is or was. It was banned by the Council and its members were all jailed or put under house arrest for sedition. I'm surprised they're still alive. The Protector is a wily bird. He's keeping them breathing to avoid a public revolt but he's pretty much pulled their claws." *(Howard didn't know that at the moment, the wily Protector was quite dead as was Peregrine.)*

Octavius replied. "We need to determine whether Ezra is ready, willing and able to restrain the hotheads who might want to start an attack on Earth or Gaea."

"It's a possibility but at the moment, I don't think they have the capability. This is going be a long, drawn out affair. I doubt if we'll get any help from General Turmoil. I'm sure he'd like to leave the exoplanet a smoldering wreck."

Otto piped up, "Well, he darn near succeeded. The Protector's and Council's fault of course with a strong assist from our old buddy, the late and unlamented Caleb. I know Ezra is trying to track down the Council members. They seem to have skedaddled, if they're not dead."

*****

Otto "zapped" to the Praesidium just in time to discover that the Protector's and Peregrine's dead bodies had been found by the leaders of the mob. They had been dragged out to the Plaza and shown to the shrieking members of the horde. "Death to the Council. Ez-rah, Ez-rah!"

Howard arrived and joined Otto. They stood behind two ornamental pillars flanking the Plaza, watching with avid interest. Ursula 12 was recording the event.

The Eagle flew down and confronted the throng. "Listen to me, fellow citizens. I and my party members did not cause or authorize the death of these two villains. We will seek out and capture the other members of the Council and their minions and bring them to justice – not violence but a rational trial. They must bear responsibility for the disaster that has befallen our Home World but they will be judged fairly and legally. Do you support me in this?"

"Ez-Rah! Ez-Rah! Ez-Rah! Ez-Rah! Ez-Rah Ez-Rah!!"

"Alright, I am forming a group to head up reconstruction. I call for volunteers with salvaging and repair skills. Our Earth friends are handling the technology, putting our information systems back in order and removing all the damage that was done by the cyberwarriors. They, by the way, have also disappeared."

"The police and what is left of the Army are on alert to prevent looting and once the hospitals are active again, they will be handling the accident and emergency victims. We will disband the Secret Police. They have no role to serve in the new free Home World. Our transportation facilities are currently down. As individuals, you will have to make your way by wing power. However, restoration of the movement of goods and equipment will be a first priority."

"Ez-Rah! Ez-Rah! Ez-Rah! Ez-Rah! Ez-Rah! Ez-Rah!"

"The Praesidium is locked down and will not be reopened until a provisional government is formed and plans for election are made. That will be a troublesome but necessary task requiring good will and a desire to put the welfare of all our citizens first. I will not stand for election or use our emergency situation for my personal benefit. And now, my fellow citizens, as soon as our television and social media are restored, I will address the entire planet repeating what I have said to you. Meanwhile, go back to your nests and aeries and tend to your frightened chicks."

"Ez-Rah! Ez-Rah! Ez-Rah! Ez-Rah! Ez-Rah! Ez-Rah!"

Howard, through Ursula, sent a message to Condo. "Can you send a couple of your experts out here to speed up the tech recovery? The sooner we mitigate the cyber damage, the more stable this place will be. And we can leave."

The Condor agreed and had Li-Ping arrange for several telecom and computing specialists to be quantum transported to the Capital City.

Octavius contacted General Turmoil but there was no agreement to help fix the destruction. Mattingly had "gone off the grid" and given their past history, the Horse was reluctant to send any other members of his staff to an exoplanet that had strong memories of his attacks. No joy there!

It wasn't clear what sort of reception the Octavian and UUI folks were going to get when the birds realized they came from Earth and even more serious, Octavius Bear's domains. Howard had Marlin standing by to return all the restoration crew to the Bear's Lair the moment there was any sign of hostility. They needed to talk further with Ezra.

Howard tracked down the Eagle who was surrounded by members of his Home World Free party and a number of low level officials - mayors, heads of government departments, businesses and institutions - all sorely aggrieved.

First, they wanted their systems restored which Ezra assured them was in the works. Then, they wanted to know who was responsible. The Eagle hedged, telling them only it was a plot approved by the Protector and Council to wreak havoc on Earth. It "boomeranged" doing major destruction on Home World instead. Then came the big question. News was circulating of the Protector's and Peregrine's death coupled with the disappearance of the Chancellor and Council. Was Ezra responsible?"

"No, my friends! I was under house arrest as were my associates. I believe members of the Praesidium Guard did away with the Protector and Peregrine and we don't know what happened to the Chancellor. We believe he is hiding away on Gaea. We are currently searching for the Council members and will have them arrested."

"There is also a Great Horned Owl named Mattingly who developed the technology for the cyberattack. He, too, is missing. We don't know where he came from. We'll hunt him down." *(Lots of luck!),*

Howard had Ursula transmit all of this back to Octavius. The Great Bear was becoming increasingly wary but had promised himself and the Octavians that they would restore the exoplanet's technology. Howard confronted Ezra. "It sounds like a little revenge is the order of the day."

The Eagle responded. "After all the carnage, it is difficult to assuage the tempers of an outraged populace. Anger runs deep here in Home World. I know you are from Earth and we suspect that planet was involved in creating this disaster. I don't believe you and your associates were responsible. Why is it that you are helping us?"

"Because we knew of the Chancellor's plans and plot. He came from Earth after doing the same thing to the establishment of Octavius Bear, my boss."

"Octavius Bear!? He was responsible for the death of two of our heroes."

"Two of your heroes who were intent on firebombing his home, his family and his industrial complex. Their deaths were self-defense. We have great reason to be angry with your government but we did not create this catastrophe. Peregrine has already paid for his participation. The Chancellor is missing but much of the blame rests with him. Now, do you want our help or not?"

"Yes, we don't have the capabilities ourselves."

"Alright, we are continuing to restore your systems, applications, data and networks. We will leave as soon as we are finished. The rest of the cleanup is up to you. We expect you to preserve our safety while we are here. Agreed?

"Yes!"

In the meantime, it was decided to send Otto back forthwith.

Chapter Twenty Three

Our brave Otto has once more returned
And he's downing a drink that he earned.
But the jury's still out.
The whole group is in doubt.
Will our offers of help yet be spurned?

(The Bear's Lair)

One more landing *(or controlled crash)* by the Magnificent Otter in the Multiverse Lab. "Honey, I'm home!"

Marlin called Octavius, the Frau and Colonel. "He's back!"

They descended on the room and helped him to his feet. The Frau handed him a bowl of fermented kelp juice, his favorite, and said, "So, little Otto, are you OK?"

"Let me get a couple of gulps of this ambrosia down and I'll be fit as the proverbial fiddle. Yeah, I'm fine. He looked at his laptop. You alright, Ursula? Which one are you, 12 or 13?"

"12! 13 is tied up unlocking ransomware. She's a real speed demon. It's those quantum computer modules of hers They resolve crypto like lightning flashes. She'll probably have the whole place sorted out in a few more hours. I've got all the denial of service overloads cleaned out. Next we have to activate the backups and bring all the systems and apps back on line. They have a type of Cloud that we still have to sort out but it's no big deal. Nevertheless, Mattingly and the General's techies did a real number on those birds."

Octavius nodded. "No doubt. General Turmoil doesn't believe in half measures. So, Otto, your opinion. What's our next step?"

"I'm not comfortable with the situation, Doctor Bear. That exoplanet is on the verge of global riots. I give Ezra a fifty-fifty chance of controlling the hotheads. We're getting the technology working again so that should take some of the pressure off but this is giving some of the troublemakers plenty of ammunition. Even though we're helping to restore their world, the fact that we're from Earth can trigger some pretty irrational activity. Let's get out of there ASAP."

"Colonel, how many folks do we have there?"

"Six - Howard and the volunteers from the Hex. We're on standby to lift them all the minute Howard or any of them spots any trouble."

"How long will it take to get them out?"

"Only a few seconds."

"Good, please stay alert. Those birds can be dangerous."

"How much longer will it take you, Ursula 13, to unlock those files and systems."

"Less than an hour, Doctor Bear. We're cleaning them up super quick and turning them back to the Home World techies. My quantum computing support back at the Hex is working overtime. No pun intended."

"Great stuff, those electrons and protons."

"Qubits on parade!"

The Development of Civilization Volume 15
Part 5
Quantum Computing

From *"An Introduction to Faunapology"*

by *Octavius Bear Ph.D.*

In previous volumes of these casebooks (See Volumes 4 and 14, for example) we have discussed various phenomena and characteristics of the quantum universe. "Strange" doesn't begin to describe it. We are dealing with quantum mechanics, the scientific principles addressing the infinitesimal.

Somewhere between the very, very small and the unimaginably large, there is a major disconnect among the theorists. Quantum mechanics and Newtonian physics don't match up! There have been many attempts to patch over the gaps. In the process, the theoretical multiverse has acquired as many as eleven dimensions including space - time.

There is one principle of quantum theory that should interest us at this point in our narrative. Quantum superposition at the sub-atomic level.

In 1935, a cat named Schrodinger showed how superposition would operate in the everyday world. As long as we do not observe or measure it, a subatomic object can exist in any number (a superposition) of states. It is only when we turn our attention to the object that the superposition is lost, and the object appears in only one of its potential states.

One of these objects is the fundamental component of QC (Quantum Computing)- the Qubit.

*We are all familiar with the Bit – the basic element of all of our conventional computing devices. A Bit is the fundamental stuff on which computer design is based – the binary 1's **or** 0's found in electronic* *storage and processing devices such as the transistor. All electronic digital data is nothing more or less than a string of bits. (Bytes are multiple bits packaged together.) Programs are specialized bit strings designed to provide instructions to digital devices - computers, phones and other communication devices, robots, watches, sensors, special purpose industrial, medical, entertainment machines and the like. We are immersed in bits and bytes.*

*But along comes the Qubit. It has one exceedingly important difference from its predecessor. It can represent a 1 **and** a 0 at the same time. Quantum mechanics, somewhat miraculously, enables the qubit to be in a "superposition" of both states simultaneously, a property which is fundamental to quantum mechanics and quantum computing.*

Subatomic elements can be in a binary superpositioned state in different ways: for example, the spin of an electron in which the two levels can "spin up and spin down" or the polarization of a single photon in which the two states can be the "vertical polarization and the horizontal polarization." In conventional systems, a bit would have to be in one state or the other. Not so with the Qubit. It can be both.

So what? It sounds like a physicist's, mathematician's or computer geek's play toy.

It's much more than that! There are classes of problems and processes so extensive and involved that today's bit-based, classic computers have no hope of dealing with them successfully. Some have been estimated to take thousands of years using conventional hardware and software. The term Quantum Supremacy was coined to describe situations where. by dealing with all potential paths at once, Qubit driven hardware and software would render possible applications that would forever be beyond the legacy system's ability.

Here's a short list of environments where some of these possible applications exist. Clearly, not every problem in these arenas requires Qubit design. Bit based systems are already making great contributions.

- *Cybersecurity*
- *Artificial Intelligence*
- *Computer Animation and Simulation*
- *Drug Development and Genetic Research*
- *Weather Forecasting and Climate Change*
- *Financial Modeling*
- *Energy Forms including Batteries*
- *Traffic Optimization*
- *Differential and Integral Calculus Computations*

We must quickly add that most of these QC apps are in their infancy.

OK, what makes Quantum Computing so swift and capable when it can be applied. (Which is not always the case.) In a nutshell, rather than having to perform tasks sequentially, like most traditional computers, quantum computers can run vast numbers of parallel computations at very high speed. Obviously, the problem to be solved must lend itself to this structural parallelism. Not all applications do, so quantum computing is not the answer to every IT manager's prayer. Don't ditch your current systems, some of which are already designed to run parallel processes but not at the speed, complexity and scope of QC. Think coexistence.

*Another fly in the technological ointment is the fact that today's Quantum devices are notoriously unstable. Error rates are high due in part to the nature of quantum indeterminacy. The device must <u>maintain</u> dual state superpositioning -1 **and** 0. Otherwise it will fall back to a single state – 1 **or** 0 and behave like a conventional bit driven system.*

Today's quantum prototypes are quite sensitive to physical interference and errors are more frequent than desired. There are error correction algorithms and design changes that are being developed to hopefully deal with the issue.

There are many opinions about the future of QC. Sceptics abound but the enthusiasts are also numerous. The major question is once stability is achieved and commercially viable devices are possible. if ever, what are the research, military, education and military markets? Can Quantum devices be effectively embodied in aircraft, vehicles, ships, weather stations and the like that can make use of the high speed, superpositioning phenomena or will they remain semi-experimental oddities?

Finally, what does all this have to do with encryption and decryption – Ursula 13's specialty?

Cryptosystems protect an immense number of private and secret communication programs, files and protocols, from email, financial and defense data to internet retail transactions. Current encryption standards rely on the fact that no one yet has the computing power to test every possible way to discover the correct encryption key and descramble the data once it is encrypted, but a mature quantum computer could try every option within a matter of hours or less depending on the strength of the encryption.

That's what our girl is doing in our story with a little help from her friends at the Advanced Super Computing Center (The Hexagon). The jury will be out for quite some time on Quantum Computing. We imagined it was stable and successful to move our casebook's plot along.

Chapter Twenty Four

The Plaza filled with a hostile crowd.
Their calls for Ezra were strong and loud.
Our Hex team was scared.
Then the Eagle declared
No further violence would be allowed.

(Home World)

Things were getting more and more volatile on the Praesidium Plaza. The mob had the bodies of the Protector and Peregrine Falcon and were attempting to string them up on lampposts. A search was out for the remaining members of the Council and two had been caught-the Ministers for Finance and Energy. Ezra was trying in vain to quiet things down and save their lives. It wasn't working. He flew up to his perch on the statue and shrieked.

"My fellow citizens…"

"Ez-Rah! Ez-Rah! Ez-Rah! Ez-Rah! Ez-Rah! Ez-Rah!"

"My fellow citizens! Do you want me to lead and form a transitional government?"

"Ez-Rah! Ez-Rah! Ez-Rah! Ez-Rah! Ez-Rah! Ez-Rah!"

"Then this violence must stop. Some of you raptors must restrain your thirst for vengeance. That's what got us into trouble in the first place."

A screaming female shouted, "They got us into trouble. Kill the idiots."

"Kill them! Kill them! Kill them! Kill them"

They rushed at the Councilors.

The Eagle shrieked again. "Stop! Stop now!

"Ez-Rah! Ez-Rah! Ez-Rah! Ez-Rah! Ez-Rah! Ez-Rah!"

Howard had managed to stand hidden in a niche on the Plaza. Given the mood the horde had developed, a porcupine didn't stand much chance of being accepted peaceably. The Eagle looked like he was losing what little control he had. The hotheads were in charge. The Porcupine took up his laptop.

"OK, everyone, I think it's time we headed back to Earth. Ursulas, what's your status?"

AGI 12 responded, "I've done my job. Where it's functioning, network traffic is back to normal levels."

Ursula 13 replied. "One or two more backups to decrypt and I'm a 'go.'"

"How about you Hex volunteers?"

Several voices. The consensus: "Let's get the hell out of here."

"Alright! Howard to Earth. Colonel, Marlin, bring the Hex team back NOW."

"Roger! Stand by! Activating! Whoosh! How about you, Howard?"

"I'll stay here for the moment and let Ursula 13 wrap up. If I can, I want to talk with Ezra."

The Eagle was still trying to calm the mob. With the exception of a few fierce demonstrators, he was finally having some success. They started to break up and move off, leaving the bodies of the Protector and Falcon hanging from the lampposts. Associates of Ezra were moving through the crowd urging them to leave. The two Councilors were still very much alive but being held captive.

Ezra's keen eyesight picked up a shadow in a Plaza niche. Howard! He flew down from his perch and stealthily moved over to the Porcupine's hiding place.

"Hello, friend Howard, things are barely under control. What can you tell me?"

Ursula 13 had rung her chime and signaled that she had finished her work.

"Your systems and networks have been restored. It's up to your IT staffs to get them all activated and fully functioning. My partners have left for Earth and I will be departing momentarily. This whole fiasco was the result of a paranoid thirst for revenge that badly backfired. I don't know what your personal plans are but I hope you will have a restraining effect on anyone who wants to reignite that insane desire. Chancellor Caleb has a lot to account for."

"Where is he?"

Howard lied. "I don't know. I thought your police might have tracked him down by now. He left Earth after attempting a similar attack on our infrastructure. He's clearly mad and very dangerous. *(He's also dead but we're keeping that to ourselves.)*

"Where is the Owl? We need to capture him."

"I wouldn't try, if I were you. He is very carefully protected, clever and quite formidable. Concentrate on getting Home World back to a peaceful normal. That's quite a job but I'm sure you're up to it. I realize you don't want to be the next Protector but you need to exert leadership."

"There won't be a next Protector or Council, for that matter. We're going to restructure around democratic forms."

"Well, we'll come back on occasion and see what progress you've made. I wish you the greatest success. Marlin, ready when you are!"

"Who is Marlin?

He never got an answer. The Porcupine had disappeared.

Chapter Twenty Five

Is the Home World all settled? Who knows?
Caleb's floating in space, I suppose.
But you never can tell
Where a new threat will jell,
As we bring this long tail to a close.

(The Bear's Lair)

All hands landed back at the Multiverse Lab from Biosphere X safely and secure. Belinda invited the Hexagon Team to join us for dinner *(A Frau Schuylkill spectacular)* where they were bombarded with questions by the Cubs.

The Furballs were overwhelmed by the idea of possibly working with the technologists of the Advanced Super Computing Center. They chattered away about their game and their plans for future versions. Some of the team were gamers and were fascinated by the technical sophistication these kids were demonstrating. A few promises of interest and support were made and the Cubs were ecstatic.

Octavius allowed this to go on for a while but then turned toward Otto and Howard. "Are we about to see a new, friendly Home World?"

Howard was optimistically hopeful. Ezra seemed to be a good bet. Otto was more pessimistic. "The next few month will tell a tail about the directions they take. There are factions galore on that god-forsaken rock. Tough to tell how much infighting will go on. Actually, the situation may ebb and flow for long while. We need to keep a watch on them."

"And do what if they go astray?" This from Chita.

"I don't know. It depends on what their intentions are."

Octavius said, "I called the General again and told him how we had participated in the cleanup. He was less than enthusiastic. If he had his way, he would have totally destroyed that exoplanet. He believes we will be bothered by them yet again. I'm not sure I don't agree with him. We'll see. By the way, Mattingly has taken off to the North Woods but we may yet hear from him."

Otto sniffed, "That Owl is a clever so-and-so; a technical genius and a skilled liar. I'm glad he's on our side. I hope he stays there. You were a mercenary, Colonel and you were an experimental animal with the General. What do think?"

"If the General keeps him on a generous payroll and they don't have a falling out *(which is possible but not likely)* we won't have to worry about him. But I admit, he can be ruthless, especially with imbeciles like the Protector and the Peregrine. I wonder how he and Caleb would have hit it off."

The Great Bear laughed. "Two technical geniuses, both with a major streak of malevolence. But I think Caleb's fantastic ego would have killed off any cooperation between them. Anyway, it's academic with the Cassowary's body floating out among the satellites. That reminds me. Byzantia seems to have done wonders with the new Ursula 13."

Howard agreed, "She's not finished yet. Those Quantum Computing circuits aren't fully mature. She could become unstable if she relied on them exclusively. Plus, I think we all have a deep affection for Ursula 12."

Frau Schuylkill nodded her head. "Of all of them, she's my favorite. Don't let the Condor retire her, Herr Bear."

"I won't. I share your feelings about Ms. Twelve. I don't know about all of you but I could use a healthy cask of mead."

Once again, Ilse beat Huntley to the punch with her *Höchstgeschwindigkeit (hyperspeed)* and presented the Bear with the bees' ambrosia.

"Thank you, Frau. What about you, Bruce. Back to Lyon?"

"Right, Ocko. Interpol calls. Glad we got this mess on the road to settlement. I'm with Otto. I think those birds are still a menace. If I were a Gaean, I'd be watching my back. They're an easier target than we are. They were Caleb's follow up objective. I hope we don't have another incident to clean up. I'm not sure how General Turmoil feels about Gaea but if has to cut the birds down again, he'll go to extremes."

Belinda shrugged, "As if he didn't this time."

"True, Bearoness, but next time there may be nothing left to salvage."

"Ouch! Chita, thanks for coming over. Once again, you escaped Multiverse travel. Just as well! Your Media Business is going great. The Cubs are absolutely in love with you. You've put them and their games on the global map."

"And I'm in love with them, Belinda. They're little geniuses. Actually, not so little any more. How do you handle them, Mlle Woof?"

"Carefully, Madame Catt, carefully. But they keep me young."

"Jaguar Jack, is your handicapping program ready for prime time?"

"Just about, Octavius. Deep Date Analysis is maravilloso. Think what we could do with Quantum Computers. My one failure is with Señora Chita."

The Cat laughed, "That's one race you're not going to win, Jack."

The Great Bear chuckled. "Maury, I think I'm going to wrap it up for the night. Do you have anything for me before I do."

"Nope, the decks are clear."

Belinda looked at Octavius and said, "There's something I want to discuss with you. I'll grab a bowl of champagne and we can go upstairs and talk."

Epilogue

Belinda reveals a surprise
With a wink from her large polar eyes.
She makes bold to inquire
If they both should retire.
Once again she appears worldly wise.

(The Bear's Lair - Bearonial Suite)

"What did the Cubs do this time?"

"It's not the Cubs, although they're not Cubs any more. They're really juveniles. It's us."

"Ohmigod, you want a divorce and you're going to run off with Preston Pavel Polar."

"Stop being silly. We need to think seriously about this."

"Alright, Bel. What's on your mind.?"

"I think it's time we both retired."

"When you had your recent review with Griselda, the officers, directors and managers, it occurred to me that they had everything in Universal Ursine Industries pretty much under control. Business was growing. With the exception of the Caleb induced lawsuits, there are very few downsides. What a perfect opportunity to step aside, relax, travel with Arabella and McTavish and just enjoy life."

(Clearly she was concerned about Home World inspired assassinations.)

"No more criminals, cranks or despots. You can become a 'Consulting Detective Emeritus'. We can spend more time at Polar Paradise but of course, we won't give up the Bear's Lair and we can go to fun places. There's a lot of world out there I want to see, to say nothing of other worlds. I've never quantum jumped and I'd like to."

Octavius sat with his mouth open. "Wow!"

"Tavi, is that all you have to say. Wow?"

"Frankly, my dear, I've never considered retiring."

"I know. You believe you're indispensable. The Ursine in Universal Ursine. The Octavius at the head of the Octavians. But Maury, Howard, Marlin, Otto, the Wolves and Condo all are super capable. The Ursulas are wonders and getting more so every day. Chita, the Colonel and Bruce are fabulous. Huntley and Ilse have the Lair running like a well-oiled machine. Dougal and his staff along with Lord David and Dancing Dan manage Polar Paradise to perfection. Tavi, we're not getting any younger. I'm tired of being a sidekick Bearoness and frankly, I'm bored stiff with the Aquabears. Let's do something different."

"What about the Cubs, excuse me, the Juveniles?"

"They can turn their games over to the Hexagon team and come along with us as we roam the world. They'll love it. We'll take over. Poor Mlle Woof can stay here and relax. Well, what do you say?"

"The idea has its appeal, I'm bored, too. This last round with Home World, Caleb and General Turmoil really flattened my fur. Tell you what, Bel. Let's sneak up on it. We'll take a sabbatical-one year-and see what we think at the end. An experiment. No bridges burned. The bad guys will still have the Octavians to contend with. No permanent farewells. No cold turkey, whatever that means. Things won't be exactly the same when we come back but we could resume, if we want to. We'd still own all the assets and titles. How about that for a start?"

"OK! It's my idea but I must admit to having a few trepidations, too. Slow and easy! We can keep our home bases here and in the Shetlands. I'll take full possession of the Concorde SST. Let's see if the Flying Tigers are up to being global wanderers."

"Well, it sounds like we have an announcement to make."

THE END – Volume 15 – A Case for the Birds

About the Author

Harry DeMaio is a ***nom de plume*** of Harry B. DeMaio, successful author of several books on Information Security and Business Networks as well as the fifteen-volume ***Casebooks of Octavius Bear.*** He is also a published author for Belanger Books and the MX Sherlock Holmes series edited by David Marcum. A retired business executive, former consultant, information security specialist, private pilot, disk jockey and graduate school adjunct professor, he whiles away his time traveling and writing preposterous books, articles and stories.

He has appeared on many radio and TV shows and is an accomplished, frequent public speaker.

Former New York City natives, he and his extremely patient and helpful wife, Virginia, live in Cincinnati (and several other parallel universes.) They have two sons, living in Scottsdale, Arizona and Cortlandt Manor, New York, both of whom are quite successful and quite normal, thus putting the lie to the theory that insanity is hereditary.

His e-mail is hdemaio@zoomtown.com

You can also find him on Facebook.

His website is www.octaviusbearslair.com

His books are available on Amazon, Barnes and Noble, directly from MX Publishing and at other fine bookstores.

Lightning Source UK Ltd.
Milton Keynes UK
UKHW030726051221
395094UK00005B/115